DEATH BY EGGPLANT

Susan Heyboer O'Keefe

SQUARE
FISH

Roaring Brook Press
NEW YORK

SQUARE
FISH
An Imprint of Macmillan

Square Fish and the Square Fish logo are trademarks of Macmillan and are used
by Roaring Brook Press under license from Macmillan.

Library of Congress Cataloging-in-Publication Data
O'Keefe, Susan Heyboer
Death By Eggplant / Susan Heyboer O'Keefe
p. cm.
Summary: Eighth-grader Bertie Hooks has to keep his dream of becoming a
world-class chef a secret, especially from his mortal enemy, Nick Dekker, and when
they both get "flour-sack babies" to take care of for a week, things become even
more complicated for Bertie.
[1. Babies–Fiction. 2. Schools–Fiction. 3. Cookery–Fiction. 4. Bullies–Fiction]
I. Title.
PZ7.O41445De 2004
[Fic]–cd22   2003017846

ISBN: 978-0-312-60241-3

Originally published in the United States by Deborah Brodie Books,
an imprint of Roaring Brook Press
Square Fish logo designed by Filomena Tuosto
Book design by Jennifer Browne
First Square Fish Edition: 2010
10 9 8 7 6 5 4 3 2 1
www.squarefishbooks.com

More thanks than I can say go to my agent, Steven Chudney, and my editor, Deborah Brodie.

I also thank everyone who read *Death by Eggplant* while it was still unreadable and who gave me invaluable help in bringing the book to life.

Special thanks to Bonny Becker, Susan Taylor Brown, and Laura Purdie Salas for giving me Bertie's heart.

And the biggest thanks of all to Laura Spinella, who so generously gave me Cleo.

For Laura,
who'll always be Laura Catherine to me

DAY ONE

"And for his extraordinary culinary skills, the world's first-ever Nobel Prize in Cooking goes to— Bertram Hooks!"

It was last-period math, with summer vacation close enough to touch. My daydream was just getting to the part where the cute cooking groupies show me around Stockholm after the awards dinner. Then Mrs. Menendez's voice went up a notch, and the groupies vanished. Algebra could scare anyone away.

The incredible chef Jacques Pépin was only thirteen, my age, when he began his cooking apprenticeship, but that was France. They knew what was important over there. Over here, they believe in stupid things like taking algebra, graduating from junior high, and then enduring four more years of physical, mental, and emotional torture.

"I said, 'Mr. Hooks?'" Mrs. Menendez repeated.

Without opening my eyes, I guessed.

"*X* equals 42?"

"Mr. Hooks."

Mrs. M. was holding a brown paper bag. It was bigger than a lunch bag, unless you were a jock who ate multiple hoagies and a first grader every noon.

"What is it?" I asked. I didn't remember any math problems involving brown paper bags, but it might have been a trick question.

Mrs. Menendez smiled her very special I'm-so-pleased-with-myself smile. That usually meant I was in big trouble. The expression made a creepy combination with her everyday uniform of navy skirt, navy jacket, white shirt, and navy tie. Before coming here, she must have worked in a prison. And she must have smiled that same smile at the prisoners.

"Why, it's your baby, Mr. Hooks. I believe it's a girl. Please come and take her."

"Oooooh, Aunt Bertha has a baaaa-by!" Nicholas Dekker cooed.

Nick Dekker and I were what you would call mortal enemies. Had been ever since kindergarten. Once, he had mouthed off so badly, the teacher had taken away his job of clapping erasers and given it to "that nice polite boy, Bertie Hooks." That was when Dekker decided he hated me. I had done my best to ignore him over the years. Then he twisted my name from Bertie to Bertha.

Now he cooed again. "Ooooh, Aunt Bertha and her bay-yay-by."

"That's enough, Mr. Dekker," Mrs. Menendez warned. She held the bag out toward me.

"Mr. Hooks?" she said impatiently.

"There's a baby in the bag?" I asked.

She didn't answer. She only smiled and waited.

From my seat in the last desk of the last row, the walk to the front of the room seemed longer than usual.

"Very good, Mr. Hooks," she said, when I was at her side. "Here she is."

She opened the bag and carefully tilted the contents into my hands. Out fell a squarish white package, soft, much heavier than I expected, and powdery to the touch.

"Is this a joke?" I asked. "It's a five-pound sack of flour."

"This is not a joke," Mrs. Menendez said. "It is your brand-new baby girl. Now then, Mr. Hooks, today is Wednesday. Your little bundle here will be in your care for the next ten days, till the end of the final marking period."

Mrs. Menendez gently stroked the top of the flour sack.

"In that time," she continued, "you are not to let her out of your sight—ever. When I take attendance, I'll be taking *her* attendance, too. If *she's* not here, I won't consider you here. When I see you outside of school, I'd better see her. And when the assignment is over, she must be returned in perfect condition. Do you understand me?"

This was like a bad sitcom. Heck, there are even books about flour-sack babies. Why couldn't I just read one of those books and write a report on it?

Mrs. Menendez sat back at her desk and began to thumb through her math text, ready to move on. I started to panic.

"This is all because I let Harry escape last week, isn't it?"

Harry was Miss Rogers's newt. Miss Rogers used to teach second grade, then was promoted this year to junior high. She thought it would be cute to have a class pet for science. Last week I had taken Harry out of his bowl to teach him little newt tricks, like how to roll over and beg. I guess I forgot to put the lid back on, and Harry ended up learning how to play dead. I wondered if Miss Rogers had asked to be transferred back yet.

"Poor Harry," Mrs. Menendez murmured. "Yes, it's about Harry, and it's about the Spanish vocabulary words you should have memorized this weekend but didn't—"

"But—" I had been practicing my pastries.

"—and it's about the biography of Enrico Fermi you were assigned to write for English class, but which you changed on your own to Santa Claus so you could make it all up—yes, I heard about that—"

"But—" I wanted to protest that Santa was a major force in American culture. Somehow I didn't think she would buy it.

"—and it's about the math work you promised to bring Indra Sahir in January when she broke her leg, but which you forgot to—"

"But—" I felt myself turn neon pink. *Forget* to go to Indra's? It would be easier to forget how to breathe. Three separate times this winter, I trudged nine and a half blocks, past countless leafless trees, past snow-covered houses on wide snow-covered lawns, past collies and shepherds and Rottweilers, all out on their own for a quick icy wee, and stood outside Indra's house, shivering, and not just from the cold. All the years we were in school together, I had never really talked to her. What if she invited me in now? What if she didn't invite me in? What if she said, "Who are *you*?" after I had silently worshiped her for so long?

"—and it's about the extra credit you nagged and nagged and *nagged* me for," Mrs. M. went on, "then ended up not even trying, and it's about the—"

"All right," I said. "I think I see a pattern here."

"It's really about your just being born, Bertha."

Mrs. Menendez pointed another warning at Nick, but talked to me.

"Well, you wanted extra credit, Mr. Hooks. This is it. And this time you'd better do it. I believe you have a few academic areas that could use help."

What she meant, though she didn't know it, was that I'd had a better-than-average cooking year, devoting hours and hours to technique, craft, and original recipes. Unfortunately, since there are only twenty-four hours in a day, this also meant a worse-than-average school year. I was just getting by in most subjects, doing worse in

Spanish, and outright failing math. Coincidentally, these were the two classes I had with Mrs. Menendez, plus homeroom. At least homeroom wasn't graded, though I suspected that, even now, a suggestion in her eerily perfect penmanship was sitting in the principal's in-box.

"Take care of your baby for ten days," she continued, "bring her back unharmed, and I'll add . . . three points each to your math and your Spanish grades. Miss Rogers has agreed to do the same for science. She thinks you need a lesson in responsibility."

"Miss Rogers would do that for me, after Harry?"

"What did you expect, revenge? None of us, yourself included, I'm sure, want you back here next year."

I looked down at the bag. Did I want to do it? Absolutely not! But three points each would bring Spanish and science up to my usual C. Most important, it would bring math up to a D. If I didn't do it, I faced summer school for sure, maybe even repeating eighth grade.

Not go to high school next year? It was unthinkable. How could I get early admission into the Culinary Institute of America if I had to repeat eighth grade? I bet Emeril passed eighth grade . . . Wolfgang Puck . . . Julia Child. . . .

My mental roll call of cooking greats was interrupted by a nasal whine.

"Can we all get the same extra credit?" Judy Boynton waved her hand eagerly.

With Mrs. M. as teacher, Judy's grades had nose-dived

this year, too—from A+ to A. She had cried at every report card. Now her eyes were shiny with envy as she stared at the flour sack.

"Why, yes," Mrs. Menendez said. "Everyone is eligible for extra credit. You do realize, however, that each of you has a *different* lesson that needs to be learned. Tell me, Miss Boynton, do you want me to think of a very special project, just for you?"

Thinking about what "very special" might actually mean, Judy lost that hopeful, shiny expression. She dropped her hand. "Uh, no, thank you, Mrs. Menendez."

"Good." She turned back to me. "Last chance, Mr. Hooks."

I stared at the bag.

"You'll thank me for it," she continued. "Meeting a challenge like this could mean the difference between *no* college and one of the country's best schools."

Like the Culinary Institute. Reluctantly, I nodded.

"No, don't let him have her, Mrs. M.!" Dekker pleaded. "Don't put that sweet little baby in danger just to teach Bertha a lesson. She'll never make it out alive!" Nick grabbed his throat, gagged, then fell out of his desk onto the floor. Kids gaped openmouthed. All year, Nick had been in trouble, but he had never gone this far. Maybe it was the heat. Or maybe it was the prospect of summer vacation, just two weeks away.

"That's it!" Mrs. Menendez stamped her foot. She began

to say something, changed her mind, wrinkled her brow, and thought. Suddenly the annoyance on her face smoothed out, and she smiled. "You get your own flour sack tomorrow, Mr. Dekker."

He picked his head up from the floor and shook his thick black hair away from his face. "What for? I don't need extra credit."

"You do now. Your ever-slipping grade for deportment just scraped bottom."

"But you said we'd each get a different project."

"I said you each needed to learn a different lesson. And the lesson *you* need to learn, Mr. Dekker, is that you're no better than anyone else. You're the *same* as everyone else. So you're going to get the same assignment."

"Thanks a lot, Bertha," he hissed, as I walked back to my seat. Still on the floor, he grabbed my foot and almost tripped me as I passed. "I'll remember this."

Of course he'll remember it, I thought. After all, he is my mortal enemy.

When I walked home after school, the flour sack in my knapsack seemed to get heavier with each step. Every house I passed tempted me with its neatly trimmed lawn. Each was surely home to good, decent people. I could safely leave my flour sack on its doorstep and feel no guilt. But the certainty of a failing grade kept me going.

I was surprised to find my mother's car in our driveway. My mother was a little strange, even for a parent. Mornings, she taught courses like "Uncovering the Real You," everywhere from senior centers to executive dining rooms, when some big company president needed coaching in weirdness. Three afternoons a week, she attended classes herself. Right now she was supposed to be in "Exploring Past Lives," with the emphasis on Egypt.

For my *future* life, she decided I was going to be a world-class dream interpreter. Last year she had dreamed about the number 1127, and I jokingly said it was a sign she should play the lottery. She not only won, she won $1,127. The good part was that we ate dinner out for a week. I picked fancy four-star places, took notes, and within a month, produced fair duplicates of what each of us had ordered. The bad news was that, because I had told her to play the lottery, now she thought I was going to levitate in her footsteps and be a guru like her or something.

Not guru. *"Professional see-er of possibilities"* was what she once tried to put on her tax return. My dad convinced her to change that to "lecturer and consultant."

Whatever she was, she was always busy. Wednesdays she had class, so I hadn't expected to find her home now, nor did I want her to be the first to check the mail. Stepping inside the door, I was even more surprised by the smell.

"Mom?" I sniffed the air. For a few seconds, I was confused, then I realized that something was cooking.

Something was cooking, and *I* wasn't in the kitchen. That did not make me happy.

I found her at the stove, stirring a pot so hard that goop splashed out and turned the clean enamel into a bad work of art.

"Are you okay, Mom? I mean, you're cooking. Food and all."

"Hmmm? Oh, yes dear, I'm fine." She scooped up a bit with a wooden spoon and tasted it. A baffled look crossed her face. In that moment we probably looked a lot alike. We were both tall, blond, and average looking, though my mother was much thinner. And her hair wasn't blond anymore. This month, with her past-life classes, she had dyed it red with something she called henna.

"Is it for us?" I asked. I sniffed again, hoping the answer was no. The mixture smelled like something you would use to disinfect gym socks.

"No, Bertie, it's for me," she said, waving the spoon. "This is a re-creation of an ancient Egyptian meal. It's supposed to strengthen my fledgling memories of my past life if I've done it right." She closed her eyes, scrunched up her face, and took another taste. "I think I'm getting something."

Worried, I opened the refrigerator to check that she hadn't used the makings of tonight's supper. For the main course, I was making a savory galette, which was a fancy name for an oversized tart. I found the stuffing ingredients still there—leeks, cream, and goat cheese. Good.

Satisfied, I dished out a bowlful of plain yogurt, piled some fresh strawberries in the middle, ringed the bowl with kiwi slices, and dotted the whole thing with black raspberries for contrasting color. Then I sat down at the table with my snack.

"You'll never guess what Mrs. Menendez did to me today," I said. "She gave me a baby to watch for ten days."

"A baby?" my mother repeated absently.

"Actually she said it was *my* baby."

"*Your* baby?" That got her attention. "You have a baby?"

"For the next ten days. Can you believe it? In sitcoms, the baby project is always for older kids and it never takes that long."

My mother looked around the room.

"Is the baby here?"

"Sure, it's in my backpack."

"Your backpack!"

I laughed. "It's all right, Mom. See?" I pulled out the bag of flour. During the last few minutes of class, I had doodled onto the sack a pair of crossed eyes, a pug nose, and a mouth with a tongue hanging out, drooling. I held it up. "My baby."

"Oh, how cute!" my mother said. She took the bag from me and tilted it this way and that, till it somehow found itself cradled in the crook of her arm. Then she mouthed something that looked suspiciously like "Cootchie, cootchie, coo."

I never should have drawn the face.

My mother turned to me. "She needs a name, don't you think?"

"A name?"

Her voice became thoughtful. "Ten days is a very long time for a baby to go without a name."

"Baby?"

"Well, she's *supposed* to be a baby, isn't she? How can you give her the care she needs, the care your *school project* needs," she added, squinting at me meaningfully, "without total and perfect visualization? On some level, this bag must really become a baby for you to do well. Like this, see?" My mother smiled at the bag and tickled it under its flap. "Cootchie coo."

That time she said it out loud.

"Mom?" I tried to laugh. "You're scaring me." Next she would ask what the flour sack's sign was, to see if we were compatible.

"Hmmm, a name . . . " She bit her lip in concentration. "Let's give the baby my real name. Let's call her Cleopatra."

My mother was right. Ten days was going to be a *very* long time.

DAY TWO

"Don't forget your lunch, dear."

I nearly choked on my shredded wheat. My mother hadn't made my school lunch since the second day of kindergarten.

This morning she was in full uniform, wearing a purple caftan and a red burnoose, which was a hooded thing that draped over her head and shoulders. Her eyes were outlined heavily with black and she had a gold snake bracelet high up on one bare arm.

"Lunch?" I looked warily at the brown paper bag she held.

"Yes, as long as I was making lunch for Cleo, I thought I should make yours as well."

"You made Cleopatra lunch?" I asked.

"Of course I made Cleo lunch. You didn't expect to feed the baby in the school cafeteria, did you?" She dropped a second brown bag onto the table, then tousled my hair. "What would you get her, silly? Tuna surprise?

Now, what sort of a grade would you get with that?"

This was all making my head spin. My mother had never taken such an interest in my schoolwork before.

"By the way," she added, "where *is* your sister?"

"My sister? I thought she was my baby."

"*Your* baby?" She laughed. "Bertram Hooks, you're an eighth-grade boy. The school couldn't possibly expect *you* to have a baby. So she must be your sister. Now, where is she?"

"Uh . . . in my knapsack."

"Well, that just won't do. She needs fresh air. Carry her to school. I'm sure your teacher will be watching for little things like that. Then I'll run out this afternoon and buy you one of those dear little papoose holders so you can strap her to your chest."

"Dad!" I ran from the kitchen.

I caught my father hurrying from the bathroom, buttoning his shirt with one hand, combing his blond hair with the other, all the while talking into a cell phone tucked between his shoulder and his ear. My father was tall, like my mother and me, and thin, like my mother, unlike me. It was as though two string beans had somehow given birth to a butternut squash. I guess being "stocky," as the clothing saleswoman so tactfully put it, was an occupational hazard of cooking.

"No, you're wrong," he was saying into the cell phone. "It's 14.2359 percent."

"Dad!"

He held up a hand for me to wait.

"I triple-checked the figures myself," he said. "If we use 14.2358 percent, then we might as well start selling gambler's insurance to lottery players."

My father was the head actuary at an insurance company. That meant he calculated the odds on weird things like, what were the chances that a left-handed Eskimo in a red turtleneck was going to get hit by a yellow 1990 Volkswagen driven by a Norwegian sailor on shore leave?

"Dad!" I tugged on his shirttail. "I've got to talk to you *now*! It's Mom," I said. "And it's an emergency."

"Look, Jim, I'll call you later," he said. "I've got something very important going on here." He clicked the button and gave me a tired smile. He was probably up most of the night again, suspended between his laptop and his cell phone.

Sometimes I suspected my father actually thought in numbers, the way immigrants might think in their native language. There was a three-second delay to everything as Dad translated my question into number-ese, then his number-ese answer back into English.

"What's wrong, Bert?" he asked me now.

"Did you know I have a baby sister?"

"What?" The blood rushed from his face. "You mean your mother is . . . ?"

"No, it's worse." My words tumbled out in a rush. "The

baby is really just a sack of flour from a school project I'm supposed to take care of to teach me responsibility because I let the class newt Harry escape and dry up and I do get all shaky whenever I think of him but this is ridiculous and Mom thinks I'd get a much better grade by pretending the bag is real because what sort of grade would I get if I bought it tuna surprise for lunch instead of baby mush and I thought maybe she was just getting carried away helping me but she's really gone overboard and changed the bag from a bag to my baby and then to my baby *sister* which means now it's her baby and if it's *her* baby then that also makes it yours."

"I have a baby daughter who's a newt?" He began to look woozy.

"No, Dad, listen! You don't have a real baby, you have a flour-sack baby. Mom even named it. *Cleopatra,*" I added. *Now* he would realize how serious things were.

Instead, he laughed with what seemed like relief and walked me down the hall. He stopped for a moment at the threshold of the kitchen and looked in. My mother had slipped on a pair of headphones and was singing softly to herself as she switched the contents of her purse from a small black one to a purple one that matched her caftan.

As always, just the sight of her made Dad's whole face soften and light up. It didn't matter if a troupe of green-haired circus dogs was right there juggling flaming torches. If my mother was in the same room, she was all he ever saw.

"You know, Bert," he said, speaking softly so she would not hear him over the music. "Your mother is a very special person, and she has two main jobs in life. The first is to discover the specialness in other people and to help them see that, and the second is to discover the full extent of her own specialness. Just as *your* job right now is to go to school and not worry. And mine is to take care of business, because so far, this day has an 87.77 percent chance of being a disaster." He flipped open the phone and thumbed in a number.

"But Dad, what am I supposed to do?"

"Your very best, son, just like always."

"Well, sometimes my best isn't very good," I said. "If I don't do this project, I'm going to fail math. I . . . I might even fail eighth grade." There. I had confessed.

"Fail math?" Genuinely surprised, he shut the phone and put his arm around my shoulder. "No way, champ."

Champ? Didn't he ever look at my report card when he signed it? Or did he think Cs stood for "creative," "clever," and "capable"? My mother thinks that, deep down, beneath all the piles of numbers, my father is the world's biggest romantic. I could say he was blinded by love. Sometimes I was afraid he was just inattentive.

He gave my shoulder a squeeze. "It'll pass, Bert," he said earnestly. "Whatever it is, it'll pass. I can say that with a confidence factor of 99.877 percent. That's how life is. Growing up, too. Things pass. Now go back in there and finish your breakfast. Kids who eat a hearty but healthy breakfast are five and four-sevenths times more likely to go to business school than kids who don't."

"Business school?" The phrase was old news but it popped out of my mouth anyway.

"Business school," he repeated. "Wharton. My alma mater. You'll enroll in their actuarial science program, just like me. You're gonna love it!" he said, as if he were giving me the world's best gift.

"But, Dad, what if . . . ? I mean . . . " *Culinary Institute of America*, I kept repeating to myself silently. Maybe if I thought hard enough, I could zap the words into his mind. Of course, it would be easier to just say them, but I hadn't gotten up the nerve yet.

"What if what?" he asked.

"Nothing."

"Are you sure? Hmmm?" he persisted. I shook my head. He was ready to listen. I just wasn't ready to talk. "All right, then, son," he said. "I'll see you tonight."

Could it be possible that my father was a *bad* actuary? I mean, what were the odds that a kid who was failing math and who forever had flour under his fingernails was going to grow up and enroll in an actuarial science program? My father couldn't foresee probability when it was under his own nose.

–Like when he built a pyramid on our front lawn for my mother at the beginning of her Egyptian craze. Even *I* saw the probability, and without a calculator, that the neighbors might object. And the zoning board. The only ones who didn't object were the neighborhood dogs.

–Or when Dad let me have my first kitchen blowtorch so I could caramelize food. There was a good, maybe an overwhelming, probability that at age nine I wasn't ready for it. We ended up with new cabinets, which we needed anyway, but for months, the lingering smoke gave all my recipes a barbecue flavor.

–And even way, way back, when he let my mother name me. My mother had been going for her third master's degree at the time and had been studying Middle English, which I don't quite understand, because how can English have a middle? And if it does, then where does it end? Anyway, she wanted to call me Beorhthramm, which sounded like something you would spit up during the flu.

Dad wanted to call me John.

Beorhthramm or John. This should not have been a difficult decision. After all, what was the probability that a name like Beorhthramm would later cause all sorts of legal problems because of misspellings, not to mention the personal trauma of walking into kindergarten, saying the name, and being sent to the nurse. But my mother wanted it, and my father gave in—either blinded by love again or inattentive to what was going to be my very painful reality.

Thankfully, some fourth cousin twice removed convinced my mother at my christening to forget the birth certificate and have my name changed to Bertram. When I first hit school, the worst I had to hear was, "Hi, Bert! Where's Ernie?" At least till Nick Dekker remembered his Aunt Bertha.

Dekker. He was getting his own flour-sack baby today. Which meant that today had a much, *much* better-than-87.77-percent chance of being a disaster.

Mrs. Menendez put a white sack of flour onto Nick Dekker's desk. His mouth was already open with protest when she shushed him.

"Not a word," she said, "or you'll be taking care of that baby so long she'll be your date for the senior prom."

Mrs. Menendez walked to the front of the room, folded her arms, and looked from me to Nick and back again. The room was empty except for us. After Spanish, she had kept Nick and me behind at lunch. I hoped she didn't take long, as lunchtime was usually when I did the homework I was supposed to have done the night before.

"Mr. Hooks, Mr. Dekker—please note that this is not just any brand of flour off the supermarket shelf. The labels show that these are bags of stone-ground flour from Dutch's Old-Time Oregon Mill. That means if anything happens to your babies, you cannot buy a replacement to try to fool me."

A slow smile snaked its way across her lips.

"So, in case you are thinking about neglecting your duties, then ordering an extra bag or two from Dutch," she said, "give it up now. Dutch sold his place over the winter, and it's now Granny Greta's Merry Mill. That's what the new labels say."

"Granny Greta?" Nick said. "No way. I bet I could go online anytime to this Web site." He tapped the fine print on the side of the bag.

Did he think she was bluffing? My academic life was on the line, and Dekker was playing poker, with my final grades as chips.

"But who cares about extra flour?" he said, with his own snaky smile. "I bet you can't make me do this. My dad's a lawyer, remember? You'll never get away with it!"

I sank lower in my seat. This was beginning to sound like a bad gangster movie.

"C'mon, Nick," I pleaded. "You don't talk like that to a teacher. Just take the sack and go to lunch."

"It's good advice," Mrs. Menendez agreed.

"No!"

"Mr. Dekker, I'll give you an undeserved break and tell you this: Before you do anything rash, why don't you talk to your *mother* the lawyer first? I did. She thought it was a very innovative assignment."

"You talked to my mother?" Dekker sat up straight. A bright red flush colored his cheeks.

"Of course. And I explained the situation to the principal first before doing anything. I cleared it with your other teachers as well, so that all of them are expecting to see a flour sack from each of you."

Parents, principal, teachers—Mrs. Menendez had covered everything. Dekker pounded the desk with his fist, grabbed the flour sack, then stomped out of the classroom.

"Gee, thanks, Mrs. M.," I mumbled.

"What?"

"Well, it's bad enough having to take care of Cl–" I caught myself. "This." I nudged the sack on my desk. "Now Dekker is mad, and he'll want to take it out on someone. That always means me."

"Don't be silly, Mr. Hooks. This has nothing to do with you."

I didn't even try to explain. I pulled myself to my feet, dropped Cleo into my knapsack, and walked out to the schoolyard.

Five minutes later, I was facedown in the grass. At least I wasn't a city kid, facedown in concrete.

"You know what your problem is, Bertha? Or should I say, what one of your many problems is?" Sitting on my back, Dekker whispered into my ear. "You're not even really fat, you're just *soft*." He hissed out the word. "Soft and mushy." He rifled through my knapsack, then started talking loudly so kids would gather around.

"What, oh what, does Aunt Bertha have in her purse today, boys and girls?" he asked. "Let's see. Here's our poor little flour baby. Oh look, she has a face. Isn't that cute?" He held it up with one hand, while rooting in my knapsack with the other. "And there's *this*." He shook his head. "Some people will do anything to suck up." He showed all the kids Cleo's brown bag lunch, which my mother had so thoughtfully labeled "The Baby's." I bet no one in Dekker's family would make *his* flour sack lunch. The thought of Dekker ever meeting my mother sent such a shudder through me, he must have thought I was trying to shake him loose.

He elbowed me in the back, then continued, "And lookie what's in the bag. An itsy-bitsy jar of strained prunes!"

My inner chef clucked his disapproval. *Jar food? No, no, no! Babies need organic ingredients for their brand-new little bodies.* I began to sort through my mental storehouse of recipes.

"Ooh! And here's an itsy-bitsy baby spoon to go with the itsy-bitsy jar!"

Above the hooting came one lone voice.

"I think it's funny," said Indra Sahir.

Please, no, I prayed. Of all days, why did Indra have to pick today to discover I existed?

With Indra and Nick Dekker, it had been true love for

longer than anyone could remember. Maybe that's the reason I had stood shivering outside her house with her schoolwork. Knock on her door, get my head knocked off. I was a coward twice over, nervous about Indra, nervous about Dekker.

But time had been on my side. Between Indra's bad break and the icy weather that was murder on her crutches, she was out of school two months. She had nothing to do all that time but grow. When she finally returned, instead of being eye-to-eye with her true love, she could eat peanuts off his head without even standing on tiptoe. The height difference didn't seem to bother her. Heck, if she could see good in Dekker in the first place, she wasn't going to change her mind over a few inches. But I guess Dekker hated looking up at her. He had barely talked to her since she'd come back. Not that *I* was allowed to. Ever since I had volunteered to take Indra her schoolwork, Nick's attitude toward me had worsened. To cap it off, as tall as Indra was, I was taller still.

Dekker had gone from small, wiry, and mean to small, wiry, mean—and out for blood.

And now Indra was trying to save me. Her beautiful brown face was indignant; her long black hair was a shimmering helmet and cape. I sighed. Usually the knight in shining armor was a guy rescuing a girl. I guess she didn't read the same books I did.

With a swish, Indra tossed her hair over her shoulder,

then reached out and grabbed Cleo from Dekker's hand.

"Strained prunes are just *sooo* funny," she said. "I mean, if you have to do this flour-baby thing, do it big and make a joke out of it."

The other kids wandered away, sensing a fight wasn't going to happen after all.

Losing his audience made Dekker madder. He leaned close and said, "Who packed the cute little his-and-her bags, Bertha? Your mommy? Is she still making lunch for you? Does she still wipe your big fat tush, too? Oh, I can just imagine your mother!"

No, you couldn't, I thought. Not in a million years.

"Let Bertie up," Indra said. "And give him back his prunes." She dropped Cleo into my knapsack, planted her feet, and crossed her arms.

Bertie. She called me Bertie. She knows my name.

I smiled into the grass.

Dekker growled, "I'm sick of looking at you every day, Bertha. So you can suck up all you want to Mrs. Menendez, but it won't make a difference. You're not passing this assignment. Your little flour baby is history. And so are you." He elbowed my back again, this time more sharply, then said, "You're a big soft wuss, Bertha, the biggest wuss I ever saw. You couldn't get any wussier if you tried."

Suddenly I knew there was something even worse than Nick Dekker finding out about my mother. That

something had been inches from his hand in the inside zipper pocket of my knapsack, the secret birthday present I
had bought myself at the mall a couple of months ago and
kept stuffed there for safety's sake, in case my mother was
hit with a cleaning spell.

It was the badge of my passion, all my hopes made visible, and absolute proof that it certainly *was* possible for me
to get wussier: a genuine toque or, to be less precise, a big,
white, floppy chef's hat.

DAY THREE

"How was school?" my mother asked, as she pulled into the supermarket parking lot. Friday afternoons she picked me up after class and drove me to do the grocery shopping.

"School was okay."

"What did you do?"

"Nothing much."

She nodded at my answer. Grown-ups were way too easily satisfied. Didn't they know that "nothing much" usually meant your life was falling apart?

"And how was Cleo's day?" she asked.

"Boring."

"Boring?"

"Mom, I think that happens a lot when you're a flour sack."

"Bertie, that kind of attitude will not produce a passing grade. Now, how was the baby's day? Did she behave herself?"

"No, she did not," I said. I remembered Indra's words. Maybe both she and my mother were right. If I had to get into this, I might as well get into it big. "Cleo watched me fail a spelling test and wouldn't give me a single hint."

"Bertie," Mom sighed. She pulled into a parking spot, turned off the car, and faced me. "You don't learn by cheating. Besides, you shouldn't be teaching your little sister such things."

"I'm joking," I said, rolling my eyes. "And I don't have a little sister. I have a sack of flour."

"Visualize, Bertie, *visualize*! Not a flour sack, but a baby! And jealousy between siblings is a natural part of growing up. It's very healthy for you to express it," she said with a face so straight it worried me. "It was only when I admitted to Dr. Garth my own jealousy about your Aunts Minerva and Debbie Lu that I made any progress at all."

Dr. Garth had been last year's therapist, in between some flake I used to call Sufi Master Alakazam and the current Dr. Zimmerman.

Still in the parking lot, I strapped Cleo into the shopping cart's baby seat, just in case we ran into Mrs. Menendez. My father wasn't home yet, and if I didn't have Cleo with me, Mrs. Menendez would probably want a notarized receipt from a babysitter.

Once inside the store, I explained the situation to the manager. I didn't want him thinking I was shoplifting when we tried to leave. He took one look at how my mother kept patting the top of the bag and cooing, then waved us on. "Class project—*sure*," he said.

First stop was fruits and vegetables. I often didn't decide ahead of time what I was going to cook. I had to see first what was fresh, what was ripe, what called to me softly as I passed by. Bread was a good example of the opposite of this. Bread was always waiting and ready to be made, like a faithful dog who waited for your return home each night. As long as you nurtured your yeast, bread would always be there. The thought couldn't help but tug at my heart-strings a bit, and I looked at Cleo.

But fruits and vegetables weren't like bread. They were fickle. I didn't like to arbitrarily decide on a Tuesday that on Friday I would make pears flambé. I liked to see the pears first. Were their pale green skins smooth and unblemished, free from bruises that would darken the fruit? When held and hefted, were they solid and firm, yet did they yield slightly to gentle pressure? Were they almost ripe enough to perfume the air? Only then might I decide to make pears flambé. So it was with most fruits and vegetables.

Today I wouldn't look at the eggplants, no matter how plump and purplish black they were. Nope, I wouldn't even listen to them.

And if I didn't think about eggplants, then I also wouldn't think about *that*, I told myself, steering the shopping cart out of the vegetable aisle. Nor was I going to ask my mother if any mail had come for me. After all, a watched pot never boils. I was firmly and absolutely putting all thoughts out of my mind . . . about *that*.

I headed for the baking aisle next. I needed turmeric and fenugreek seed to restock my spice rack. Exotic, yes, but I was out, and never knew when I might need them.

"How about cornbread?" my mother asked, picking up a box of ready mix with dancing corn muffins on the label. "You know how much your father loves it." She smiled to herself, as if cornbread was a secret joke between them. It probably was.

"Okay," I said. I took the box of mix out of her hands, put it back on the shelf, and instead gave her a bag of yellow cornmeal. Cornbread from scratch was so simple, they should shoot whoever decided it needed instant mix. Quickly I planned the full menu. Cornbread went well with roast chicken, another of Dad's favorites. I would fix buttermilk skillet cornbread to go with the chicken, a simple classic, always good.

Mom dropped the bag of cornmeal into the cart. I was just about to make a joke about its being Cleo's long-lost cousin, when the sound of Nick Dekker's voice assaulted me from the next aisle.

"No, I don't wanna buy that for you while you get fruit," I heard Dekker say loudly. "Why can't you buy both? Better yet, why can't I just wait in the car?"

I panicked. Dekker had left me alone all day, which

could only mean that he was busy calculating his next move. But he would never pass up a chance to get me here without Mrs. M. around.

When he stopped talking, I couldn't tell which way he had headed, and so which way I should run. What if Dekker caught me here? Where had my mother suddenly gone? And what in the world could I do with Cleo? I couldn't let Dekker find me with a flour sack strapped into a shopping cart full of baking ingredients.

Silence, then the squeak of shopping cart wheels, which spooked me to action. I grabbed the sack and shoved it onto the shelf of flour with all the other bags. Then I left the cart where it was, ran down the aisle—

—And slammed smack into Dekker. He was carrying several cans and some five-dollar bills, which I knocked right out of his hands.

The smart thing would have been to run before he saw who had bumped him. But I have never been known for doing the smart thing. Instead Nice-Guy Bertie automatically stooped to help pick up the money and cans. I read the words on one of them: *"Diet DeLite! Complete Meal Appeal!"* He grabbed the can from me.

"Watch where you're going, Bertha!" His face suddenly turned shades of red, like a Christmas quilt that forgot the green.

"Sorry." I began to back away. My mother appeared behind Dekker and began to study the encyclopedia that came a book a week with your groceries. *No, no, no, don't come over to show me,* I silently begged. *Stop visualizing! Cleo can't even read yet!*

My eyes must have bugged because Dekker started to turn to see what I was looking at. I had to get his attention *now*.

"So, Nick," I said, poking him. "Shopping, huh?"

He looked at me as if I couldn't be more stupid. "No, I'm bowling, wuss," he said. "Thought I'd use your head for the ball."

I had his attention. That was as far as my brilliant plan went.

"You know, there's a special on soft-shell crabs," I babbled. "It's a little late in the season for my taste, but, you know, a good rémoulade sauce can hide a thousand flaws. It's not nearly as hard as the name sounds, it's just that it's French and—"

Rémoulade sauce? What was I thinking?

Muttering that I better not be contagious, Dekker once more started to turn. Desperate, I grabbed his shirt collar.

"Tough stain," I said. "Laundry detergent's in aisle five."

He knocked my hand away as if I had cooties.

"Yeah? I think you left your brain there," he said.

My mother finally disappeared down the natural foods aisle. Relieved, I stepped away. But I had already pushed Dekker too far.

"Not so fast," he said. "What are *you* doing here?"

"Nothing. Bowling, like you said."

His expression turned suspicious. "You alone?"

I stuck my hands in my pockets. "Sure. Why wouldn't I be? How about you?"

"Yeah, I'm alone," he said.

I had maybe the first flash of self-preservation in my entire life and didn't contradict him. But I couldn't help looking down at the cans of diet drinks he was holding. He tossed them onto a shelf of canned vegetables as if they were red hot. His scowl dared me to say a word.

"Well, I guess I'd better be going," I said.

Before he could beat me up, I ran outside. The automatic doors couldn't open fast enough, and I almost made a new exit. I ducked round the corner and waited. People streamed in and out. Finally Dekker appeared, carrying a bag. As he headed toward the parking lot, I sneaked back inside.

I found my mother in front of the lobster tank, tapping on the glass to get their attention. She never even knew that I had left.

"C'mon, let's finish up," I said.

I led her back to the baking aisle. Mom let out a shriek. "She's *gone*!"

"Who?"

"Your sister! How could you have left her?"

"It's okay. She just wanted to take a closer look at

the flour bags," I joked. "Family reunion, you know?"

"Well, get her back," Mom said, hands on her hips, obviously not amused. "You know she shouldn't be talking to strangers."

I moved the shopping cart aside and reached for Cleo on the shelf. The space was empty. My flour sack wasn't there.

I stepped closer, looked harder. Maybe someone had pushed the sack aside to get to the cake flour or something. Or maybe someone had been looking for another brand.

Or maybe someone had bought Cleo.

I thought of all those people who had left the store while I was hiding from Dekker. Any one of them could have been a flour-sack-babynapper.

"Don't worry, I'll be right back!" I told my mother, with more belief than I felt, then raced to the checkout lines.

Let her be here, I prayed. I did *not* want to fail math. I did *not* want to go to summer school. I did *not* want to have to put flour-sack-baby pictures on milk cartons.

I began at the express line, hopping around to see what each person carried, then worked my way backward. I tried asking.

"Did you see . . . ? Did you happen to pick up . . . ? Were you looking for flour?"

Suddenly I spotted her—being held upside down as a clerk repeatedly tried to scan her bottom.

I pushed my way to the front of the line.

"I'm sorry, but that's mine," I said, reaching.

A huge hairy hand clamped shut on my wrist.

I looked up and saw a six-and-a-half-foot wall of black leather, from steel-tipped boots, to studded pants and motorcycle jacket, to the cap on a shaggy bearded head. The guy was a giant, like a super-villain from the comics, Berserker Biker Bob. Probably a hundred cows had died just to dress him.

"It's mine," he rumbled.

"No, please." I pulled out of his grip. "She's my school project. I put her down for just a minute."

"Her?" the clerk said. I felt my cheeks burn. Somewhere in my panicked dash throughout the store, I had changed Cleo from an *it* to a *her*.

The clerk snickered. He had black spiky hair, two diamond studs in one nostril, and a row of silver hoops through each lip and each ear. He made me think of that cool guy Pinhead from the horror videos. Then I saw his rock band T-shirt under his store smock—*Dead Babies*. Not a good sign. Besides, he was pointing to the face I had drawn for Cleo. His snickers escalated to snorts. "Art project, huh? Like, *yeah*. Time for extra credit, I think."

"She *is* the extra credit. Look, you can't even scan her. She's not in the system."

"Everything's in the system. Even you." He flashed the scanner and blinded me with the red light. "Big Brother is watching."

"Sure, but she won't scan. Let me have her back."

"That's mine," Berserker Biker Bob repeated. "I'm making dumplings for the old folks' home."

Dumplings? A fellow cook? No, he was probably making dumplings as a side dish to serve *with* old folks, not dumplings *for* old folks.

"Please?" I repeated.

Pinhead shrugged. He had given up scanning and was trying to enter the code manually. "It still won't come up. You need a different bag anyway," he told Berserker Biker Bob.

"But this is stone-ground," the other rumbled. "From *Dutch's Old Time Oregon Mill.*"

"I'll run back and get you a different bag," I wheedled. "Just as good for dumplings, I promise."

He shook his head. "I want *this* bag."

"No!" I said, scared enough now to grab Cleo from the clerk. Again a gigantic hairy hand closed over my wrist. Then a smaller hand with long red nails appeared from nowhere, closed over his, and squeezed hard.

"Drop it, buster!"

The three of us—Berserker, Pinhead, and me—looked up. It took me a moment to recognize my mother.

"Don't you *dare* touch my son." Her squinted eyes threw off icy cosmic rays.

Berserker Biker Bob and my mom stared at each other. I wasn't sure what happened between them in the silence, but the clerk kept looking back and forth as if following a tennis match. In the end, Bob dropped my hand and muttered an apology.

Mom reached out and took Cleo, cradled her in her left arm, and motioned for me to follow her.

On the way to the car, I found myself looking over both shoulders and scanning both the parking lot and the trees surrounding it to make sure that Dekker wasn't there.

Maybe I needed to take intimidation lessons from my mom.

DAY FOUR

"You should have seen her!" I crowed, flipping a pancake onto Dad's plate with enthusiasm. "This guy was like ten feet tall and all leather. I expected chains and whips and spikes—he was *that* scary. Mom made him crumple with just a look. She was as scary as he was. Scarier, because he backed down."

My father hadn't heard what had happened till now, since he had worked late last night, past midnight. Now he had to be on the golf course at seven. He hated golf, but sometimes the company president wanted him there to explain probability to a client. My father preferred to explain things at work. If he had two hands on a golf club, he had no hands left for a keyboard or cell phone.

That's why I usually got up early on golf mornings to make him breakfast before he left. I didn't have many other chances to talk to him. And besides, I make incredible pancakes, if I do say so myself. Too much handling, too much checking and flipping, made them tough, but I had an instinctive feel for when to make my move—when the tops dried to a weave of open bubbles and the bottoms were exactly a perfect dark gold, ringed with crispy brown. Plus I had a secret ingredient: I folded a cup of quinoa grains into the batter at the end. When you eat them, the quinoa pops in your mouth.

"'*Don't you* dare *touch my* son,'" I mimicked, trying to make my voice threatening and Momlike all at once. "And the whole time, they're holding Cleo upside down and trying to scan her bottom."

"Cleo?" Dad said, between bites. Apparently, he had blocked the memory of discovering he was a father again.

He was saved by the ringing of the cell phone.

"Yes, yes, Jake, I've got the figures on me. Projections from Plan 1, versions 3.5, 3.6, and 3.72," he said. "No, no, I won't mention a single number till at least one-fourth of the group has played the seventh hole."

"What time will you be back?" I nudged his shoulder. "Mom wanted me to ask."

"What time? No, not you, Jake, wait a minute." Dad pressed the receiver against his chest. "What?"

"Mom wants to know if you'll be back by noon. Dr. Zimmerman wants to meet us." It must have been pretty important. He was the first of Mom's therapists to ask to see the whole family.

"Dr. Zimmerman?" Dad said.

His expression was so blank I couldn't help myself.

"You know, the baby doctor for Cleo. Because she's so pale."

"Something's wrong with the baby?" He clicked the off button and tossed the phone to the side. The cell began to chirp at once. He waved at it. "I'll cancel the golf game."

"No," I said in alarm. "It's all right. It's just a joke. There *is* no baby, remember?"

"Are you sure?" he said.

"I'm sure, Dad. Ask anybody."

After he left, I put the rest of the pancake batter in the refrigerator, loaded the dishwasher, then took my math homework outside to the backyard. I had tried doing it last night as I waited for Dad, but it was late and my eyes had stung just looking at the problems. This morning it didn't look any easier. *X equaled 4ab to the power of grapefruit when X equals 666?* That didn't make sense. "Algebra" was probably just a code word for how to torture seventh and eighth graders.

My father had tried to help me with math many times, but we spoke different languages. In my head, I could multiply and divide teaspoons, ounces, cups, and quarts, and adjust any recipe to any size crowd. I just couldn't put that crowd onto two trains, both traveling north from different starting points at different speeds, and tell you which one would get to Boston first.

Math book and notebook under one arm, I dragged a

lawn chair to the middle of the yard. The day was sunny and warm, yet early enough that the grass was still damp with dew. Bees buzzed from flower to flower, humming while they worked. I opened my book, but the morning sun slanted into my eyes and forced them closed. It was a crime that school was still in session in June.

I didn't remember feeling sleepy. But the next thing I knew, something bumped my toe. The buzzing, which had gotten much too loud, suddenly stopped. I bolted up and shut my mouth, which for some reason was open.

"You were snoring."

"What?" I blinked hard, looking up into the sun.

If I was snoring, I must have been sleeping. And if I was sleeping, I must have been dreaming. Only that could explain the sight of Indra Sahir standing over me. She wore pink shorts and a pink top. Her brown arms and long brown legs looked like they had an end-of-summer tan, except it was the beginning of summer and that was their color all year long. I remembered every joke I had ever heard about my being Moby Dick, the great white whale.

"I said you were snoring," she repeated. "*Soooo* loudly. That's why I poked you. Before you attracted the bees, you know? You sounded like a big one yourself."

"A big what?"

"A big bee," she said patiently.

I finally realized that I was awake and that Indra was no dream. Well, yes, she was a dream, but I wasn't dreaming about her at the moment. I sat up straight and wiped my chin. No drool. Good.

"What are you doing here?" I asked, rubbing my eyes.

She shrugged. "Walking home from my piano lesson," she said.

"Oh."

She had walked home from piano through my back-yard? Sure. Then it hit me: She had come here deliberate-ly to see me. Indra Sahir had come to see me, Bertie Hooks. It was time to say something witty and memorable.

"I didn't know you took piano."

"For six years."

Six years? In all that time, she had never once taken this way home, not even the sidewalk out front, at least not that I had noticed, and I would have noticed. Maybe she had just moved. Or maybe she had changed teachers. Or maybe not, and she just wanted to see me. The thought made me scramble out of the chair. I dropped my math book and notebook, then bent to pick it up just as Indra did. We knocked heads, sending her black braid flying.

"Ow!" we both said at once, which somehow made it funny.

"How's the baby?" she asked with a grin.

"Not a peep out of her. I guess she's sleeping in."

"Well, it *is* Saturday."

"Yeah, Saturday," I agreed.

"Nicky's been pretty quiet the last couple of days, too."

Nicky? She called Dekker *Nicky*?

"If he's quiet, it just means he's planning something," I said.

"He's not as bad as all that," she insisted. "That's what I came to tell you—that you don't have to worry. Besides, you can handle him, I know it."

I felt myself blush. "Thanks."

Indra smiled, waved good-bye, and walked away, around the house to the street out front.

Nicky wasn't that bad? I wasn't to worry? I could handle him?

Yeah, right. And I was going to get an A in math, too.

Dad didn't come home in time from his golf game, so it was just Mom and me at Dr. Zimmerman's.

Mom went in first, while I sat by myself, the only one in the waiting room, which was really strange. Whenever I went to *my* doctor, the place was wall to wall with kids, each one green and hawking up germs of something far worse than I was there for. Dr. Zimmerman's waiting room was empty. The pale blue chairs looked as if they had never once been sat on. And there was a pile of magazines on a table, so neatly stacked I knew they had never once been opened.

I didn't touch the magazines, so they stayed in that super-neat pile. I didn't open my knapsack, either. My math book was in there, but I felt too weird to figure out problems. Besides, by this point in the year, things were hopeless. That was why I was stuck with Cleo. She was in the knapsack, too, because we didn't have a sitter.

The door to Dr. Zimmerman's office finally opened and Mom came out. Her eyes were red and she was sniffling. Before I could ask what was wrong, she waved me over to the doctor.

"Please, Bertram," he said. "I'd like to see you alone for a few minutes." The doctor was short and thin. He had rosy cheeks, curly black hair, a small beard, and a mustache with pointy ends you could twirl. It made me think he was really an elf in a suit. But he had an accent, just like a movie shrink, and I'd never heard of an elf with an accent.

He closed the door after us, pointed to the couch, then put a box of tissues in front of me.

"So," he said, when we both sat down. He smiled. I smiled. I waited for him to say something. I waited a long time. All the while, he kept smiling.

"So what?" I finally asked.

"Mmmm?"

"You said 'so' and now I'm saying, 'so what?'"

"'So what?'" he repeated. "Tell me, Bertram, why do you say that?"

I spoke more slowly. Maybe, being a foreigner and all, he hadn't understood me. "You said 'so' and now I'm saying, 'so what?'"

"Ahh," he nodded. "'So what? So what?'"

I guess he liked the phrase, because he kept repeating it.

"Don't you want to know about my mom?" I asked at last.

"Your mother? What do you think I should know about her?"

"For one thing, is there anything *I* should know?"

"Mmmm?"

"Well, I mean, she was crying just now."

"Mmmm?" Dr. Zimmerman raised a single eyebrow. "I see I must be direct, though it pains me most severely to do so. Bertram, why don't you tell me all about your baby sister."

"Sister? I don't have a baby sister."

"Mmmm? Cleo?"

"Cleo is not my sister."

"Ahhh . . . " He steepled his fingers and peeked out from between them. "Your mother said you were having a problem. Something about your losing the baby. Something about your grades being affected. Do you see how serious the problem is, that your grades should be affected?"

"Doctor, I don't think you understood what my mother meant. Cleo *is* my grade. She's just a school project."

He nodded even harder, like one of those dogs with the bouncing heads in the back window of a car. "Sometimes, it is easier to deal with difficult people by transforming them into an object," he said. "This way, we do not see their humanity. Is this not true?"

"Well, maybe."

"And so," the doctor continued, "you turn this difficult, fussy baby into your school project."

"Doctor, either there's a language barrier or my mother is getting way too wrapped up in my homework. She has only one kid—me. Cleo is a five-pound sack of flour."

"A sack of flour?" He wrote that down in his notebook.

"Yeah, she's just a future batch of cupcakes."

"Which *you* would devour, no?" Writing more furiously, he nodded so hard I thought his head would fall off.

"No! Well maybe . . . if they were chocolate. But I'd leave some for her."

"Cleo?" he said, wrinkling his forehead.

"No, my mother. She loves chocolate."

He sat back, stunned.

"You would feed your sister to your mother?" He began to write even faster. "This is classic! Straight from the Greek tragedies!"

"Actually, I came straight from home." I slid off the couch. "Which is where I think I should be going."

"And leave the issue of your sister unresolved?"

"I don't have a sister," I said slowly. "I have a sack of flour."

"You are in deep denial." He clucked his tongue and shook his head.

"Look," I said, "Cleo is outside, right now, in my knapsack."

The thought was suddenly unnerving—my mother alone with my knapsack. Visualizing Cleo, she might decide to visualize a diaper bag and dig around in it for a diaper. I didn't want my chef's hat to wind up on Cleo's bottom, with or without questions from my mother.

"You put your baby sister in your knapsack?" Dr. Zimmerman asked.

"She's not—look, just let me get her and prove it to you."

Leaning close, he spoke very gently. "Bertram, sometimes it is not therapeutic to confront reality so quickly. If you *need* your sister to be a little flour baby, perhaps there is a reason why. Perhaps it would be better for you—for *us*, yes?—if we were to look at this reason why, rather than be *shocked* by looking into an empty knapsack."

I jumped up and yanked open the door to the waiting room.

"I will *prove* it to—"

The waiting room was empty. My mother wasn't there. Neither was my knapsack.

"I guess Mom went back to the car. And she took Cleo with her."

"Why?"

"Because she'd never leave the baby here alone, of course."

"What did you say?" the doctor asked excitedly.

"I said she'd never leave—No, no, I just meant she took my knapsack with her and—"

The doctor grabbed my hand and shook it.

"A breakthrough!" he declared. "Didn't you hear it? You said 'the baby'!"

"But I–

"No! No! No!" He led me out. "Let this revelation work on your subconscious, and I will see you again in a few days. We must not lose this momentum!"

Closing the door on me, he murmured his last words, "Such a breakthrough, and in only one session!"

I would bet anything I was going to be written up for a psychiatric journal: "The Curious Case of the Boy Who Would Bake His Sister into Cupcakes."

DAY FIVE

Sunday I hung around the yard all morning, hoping Indra might walk by again. She didn't. Then it was time for church, and I dashed inside to get my tie. Mom was already dressed, wearing the kind of outfit that made people stare, something lime green with knotted sashes, topped with a turban. It didn't look Egyptian. But then again, I don't know what Egyptians wore when they weren't mummies.

She had dressed Cleo up, too, in a lacy white bonnet. Where had that come from? The thought of Mom buying baby clothes made me shiver.

She fussed with the hat. It was hard to tie the strings under Cleo's chin, since Cleo didn't exactly have a chin. Her head just ran into her feet, but no one wore a hat tied under their feet.

"It's much too hot for the strings anyway, don't you think?" Mom said. "They might give her prickly heat.

There." With a final pat, she stopped fussing. "Are you ready, Bert?"

She intended to take the baby to church.

Had Cleo been christened yet? I wondered. Would Mom ask me to be godfather? Would my godchild turn into cake batter when the baptismal water hit her? *Cake batter?* Dr. Zimmerman had planted a terrible seed in my mind. How could a budding chef be given a flour sack and not entertain such thoughts?

Sweat made my neck itch around the buttoned collar, and we hadn't even left the house.

"You know, Mom, you're right about the heat," I said, tugging at my tie. "It really *is* uncomfortable. And Pastor Werner never turns on the air-conditioning till after the Fourth of July, no matter how hot it gets. Maybe the baby should stay home."

"Your father can't come with us this week, but he won't be home, either. He has to run over to the office, so no one will be here. Cleo can't be alone, not even for a little while, Bert."

"No one will ever know," I pleaded.

"But that would be cheating. And when you get your passing grade, *you'll* know."

"You go, then. I'll stay home and babysit."

"Are you sure?" she asked.

"Sure, I'm sure." I tried to make my smile both sorrowful and sincere. "Go. I know how much you like the singing."

About as much as I *dis*liked it. The organist always made us sing the *whole* hymn. So if "Wouldst Thou Know My Wretched Name on That Final Fiery Day?" had fourteen stanzas, we would sing *all* fourteen stanzas, even if the final fiery day came while we were there.

"That is so sweet of you to stay with your sister, Bert, thank you," she said. Maybe having a flour-sack sister had some advantages after all. I was just about to rip off my white dress shirt, which was a bit too tight anyway, when my mother added, "But no, really, *you* should be the one to go. I'll stay home. If you start walking now, you can just make it."

It was better to go without Cleo than with her, so I said okay, and walked down to Good Shepherd Lutheran on Church Street.

Bobby Kim from class was there, and I sat with his family. There were so many little Kims between Bobby and his parents that they didn't notice us whispering at the end of the pew. So that was good. But all the hymns were whoppers, and the heat had really inspired the pastor to rip-roaring images of hell, so that was bad.

We were only at the second-to-last verse of the final hymn when the bells rang at First Presbyterian across the street, signaling that their service would soon start. That meant we had run a good fifteen minutes late. Desperate for fresh air, as soon as the last word was sung, I said good-bye to Bobby and the Kims and ran out the side exit.

"What's your hurry, Bertha?" I heard. "I didn't know old ladies could move that fast."

Dekker! He went to First Prez and should have been inside by now. This was divine punishment for wishing church would end sooner.

Head low, hands in my pocket, I walked past him, toward the main entrance of Good Shepherd, where groups stood on the sidewalk talking. If I had to have it out with Dekker, I figured I better have help around.

All the while, part of me nagged, "He's right. You *are* a big wuss. Punch him now!" I couldn't. So what if I towered over him? Elephants squealed at the sight of mice, didn't they?

"What do you want from me?" I asked, when I figured I was close enough to yell for help. "It's Sunday. Give it a rest."

"Why don't you make me?" he dared. "You and your little flour-sack baby. Where is the brat anyway?"

"An excellent question," we heard from the side.

Both of us turned. There stood Mrs. Menendez, her everyday uniform of navy skirt, jacket, and tie exchanged for her Sunday best: the identical outfit in gray. How could I have forgotten? Mrs. Menendez went to Our Lady Queen of Peace, up the block. There was a reason the town had named this Church Street.

"Didn't I say I wanted to see your baby with you at all times, both in school and out of school?"

"It's awfully hot out for a baby," I said. "Prickly heat, you know?"

"Is that inadequate excuse your idea of responsibility? I repeat, Mr. Hooks: Where is your baby? And for that matter, where is yours, Mr. Dekker?"

A horn tooted from across the street.

"Yoo-hoo, Bertie, yoo-hoooo!"

It was my mother calling out the car window.

No, please. Not Mom, not here, not with Dekker and Mrs. M. to see.

My mother made a wide U-turn. When she pulled up, the car bumped up over the curb with a nasty grinding sound. She left the car at that weird angle, turned off the engine, and stepped out. Sunlight hit yards of lime green all at once and I had to shield my eyes. It was as if she had plugged herself into a socket and begun to glow.

I ran the few steps to the car.

"Hi, I'm ready, let's go."

My mother didn't budge, but waved at Mrs. M.

"Hel-looo, Mrs. Menendez!" Just my luck. My mother, who was sometimes too distracted to remember what day it was, somehow managed to remember Mrs. M. out of all my other teachers from a single Parents Night way back in September. "Can I give you a ride?"

Mrs. M. shook her head. "No, thank you, Mrs. Hooks, I'm just on my way to church."

"Bertie's just come from there. It's so hot I figured he

could use an air-conditioned ride back. But Bertie," she said to me, "I thought, 'How silly! I can't take the baby without a car seat.'" My mother laughed at her own foolishness.

"Of course not. Let's *go*, Mom. *Please*."

"There were plenty of garage sales in the paper, though, even one right down the block, so while your father was still home, I raced out and got a seat. See?" She waved us all closer and pointed in the rear window. "Isn't she darling?"

There, in a rearward-facing infant seat was Cleo, bonnet and all, buckled in safely. With her stuck-out tongue and crossed eyes, she seemed to be saying, "*Nyah, nyah*, Bertie, can't get away from me!"

Figuring I was already sunk, I grew reckless.

"See, Mrs. Menendez? I *was* being responsible. I had an experienced babysitter."

"Oh, Bertie, don't call me a babysitter." Mom smoothed down my hair. "I'm Cleo's mother!"

As always, Mrs. M.'s expression was unreadable. In school, I figured it meant, "Maybe you just passed, maybe you just failed, but no matter which, I can still make life miserable for you, and I will." What did it mean here? I didn't know.

Before Mrs. Menendez could speak, from up the block, electronic bells began to peal. She checked her watch.

"I'm late," she murmured. Without another word, she

nodded her good-bye and walked up the street toward Our Lady Queen of Peace.

"See you soon," Mom called, waving again.

"Mom?" I asked. "I'm ready. Please, let's go."

I guess God was still mad that I hadn't liked the hymns because, instead of getting back in the car, my mother turned to Dekker and smiled.

"Isn't your little friend here from school, too?" she asked. "Would you like a ride?" she said to him.

Little? Did she have to use the word *little*? He would kill me now for sure.

Totally oblivious, Mom said to Dekker, "You'll have to sit in back with the baby, but I'm sure she won't mind."

And then she winked.

This meant big trouble. Grown-ups always winked before they made a joke. This was to alert you that a joke was coming, so you could be polite and laugh. And I was right. After Mom winked, she continued, "I even changed Cleo's diaper right before driving over. We wouldn't want to lose the air-conditioning by having to roll down all the windows, now would we?"

While Dekker stood speechless, my mother said, "And speaking of air-conditioning, I already turned it on at home, Bertie, so when you try out your new recipe for Dolly Madison's Lemon Lace Wedding Cake, you won't heat up the whole house."

The stunned look on Dekker's face melted into pure evil, and he smiled his snaky smile.

"Cake? Lemon Lace Wedding Cake? Mmm, sounds delicious. I guess I'll see you and Cleo in school tomorrow, Bertha. Don't forget to bring me a nice big piece of cake." He snickered. *"Wuss."*

Despite the heat, goose bumps ran up my arms and down my back. Now Dekker knew Cleo's name. He knew about my mother. And he knew I liked to cook.

DAY SIX

"Mr. Hooks?"

"Present."

"And your baby?"

"Present."

So far.

The unspoken threat hung in the way Dekker's back tightened when my name was called. It was a great way to start the week, knowing I probably wouldn't live to see the end of it.

Mrs. Menendez finished the homeroom roll and closed the book.

"Gentlemen, may I see your babies?"

Dekker took his from his knapsack on the floor. Cleo was already out. I figured it was boring being inside a dark desk all the time, so I had set her on top and let her face front. This way it was Mrs. M. she was sticking out her tongue at, not me.

Mrs. M. walked down the row and paused at Dekker's

flour sack. She nodded. Then she continued to the back of the room to my seat. She fingered a small tear at the corner of Cleo's head. She probably hadn't noticed it yesterday because it had been covered by the bonnet. The paper was doubled there, so no flour had spilled from it.

Still . . .

Mrs. Menendez made a "hmmmm" sound. I immediately wanted to defend myself. The tear had happened while I was trying to rescue Cleo from Biker Bob at the supermarket. If I hadn't acted responsibly then, Cleo would have been history. Well, not history, but certainly dumplings.

I couldn't get the words out. What if Mrs. M. asked how Cleo had fallen into the guy's evil clutches in the first place? I would have to confess that I had stuck Cleo on the baking shelf to temporarily get rid of her. It seemed so obvious now: I had hidden her, not behind the toilet bowl cleaner, but in the most vulnerable place in the entire store, with all the other sacks of flour for sale. Maybe subconsciously I *had* wanted someone to buy her. I shook my head in confusion. When was my next appointment with Dr. Zimmerman?

"This is a tear, Mr. Hooks," Mrs. M. said.

"Yes, it is. But it's very little. And all kids get bumps and scrapes, no? They try to walk and . . . and they fall down."

"This is a baby, Mr. Hooks. Your baby. Not a kid."

"Should I put a Band-Aid on it? I'd already thought of

that, but then my second thought was maybe it would heal faster if I let the air at it."

A snort came from Dekker's direction. Mrs. M. didn't turn. She stood looking down at me, hands folded behind her back.

"But if *you* think a Band-Aid is better," I babbled, "I'll bring Cleo down to the nurse during lunch and get one. Unless you think she needs stitches."

"Are you being sarcastic, Mr. Hooks?"

"No, Mrs. M."

"I was afraid of that," she answered.

"So?" I asked. "Band-Aid? Air?"

"Stitches?" asked Dekker. "Brain surgery?"

Without answering either of us, Mrs. Menendez walked to her desk, picked up the tape dispenser, and brought it back.

"This will be sufficient, Mr. Hooks."

"Thank you, ma'am."

I carefully taped the tear and returned the dispenser.

"Awwww, I hope Auntie Bertha kissed the boo-boo first to make it better." Dekker puckered his lips and made sucking sounds. "Boo-boos don't get better without kissy-poos, though I hear Lemon Lace Wedding Cake helps."

"I'd like to tape *your* mouth, Dekker."

I gulped. Had I actually said that? Out loud? In front of Mrs. M? *In front of Dekker?*

"Yeah, you and what army?"

Yep, I had said it.

"Mr. Hooks, your outburst astonishes me," Mrs. M. said, without the teeniest look of astonishment on her face. "Gentlemen, if you like, the two of you may continue your conversation this afternoon in detention." The smallest smile touched her lips. "I'm proctor all week."

Nick sullenly turned away.

The bell rang and kids dashed off to Mr. Neil's first-period English class. But Mrs. M. lifted one finger, signaling for me and Cleo to stay behind.

She studied the two of us, then said, "This assignment is not turning out quite as expected."

Maybe not for her, I thought. From the very beginning, I had expected to be squashed down to a grease spot. No surprise there.

"How is your mother, Mr. Hooks?"

"My mother?" I had been dreading the question ever since we all met outside church yesterday. "My mother is fine."

"Is she? She seems a bit . . . overly involved in your project."

"Well, she's like that," I said. "Involved. But that's what mothers do, right? Get involved? Good mothers, I mean?"

"You don't think she's stretching the definition?"

"Of being a good mother?"

"Of being involved," Mrs. M. corrected me.

Heat flashed up my neck.

"It's okay," I said.

"Do you really believe that?"

"It's not like she does my homework for me or any-thing. It's just that Cleo appealed to her, maybe because I was an only child, *am* an only—"

"Cleo?" Mrs. M. sat up a bit straighter, if that was pos-sible. "I thought that's what I heard yesterday. Your moth-er named your sack of flour, and the name she chose was 'Cleo'? Short for 'Cleopatra,' I presume?"

"It's not a sack of flour, Mrs. Menendez. It's my baby. You've told me that many times," I reminded her.

"Yes, I have."

But she looked doubtful. Mrs. M. in doubt? It would be easier to discover the world was flat after all.

"I'll finish the project by myself," I promised.

"In any case," she said, "there are only four more days left."

Suddenly I caught a glimpse of Dekker at the hallway door. The creep had stayed behind and had heard the whole thing. Now he was wearing an I'm-going-to-get-you grin.

"No, five more days, counting today," I sighed.

I managed to avoid real contact with Dekker all morning. But I figured my lunch options were going to be ketchup or no ketchup on his knuckles. When the bell rang at the end of Mrs. Menendez's Spanish class, he turned, pointed at me, then pointed toward the windows that overlooked the schoolyard. *"You, out,"* the gesture said. He stood up and swaggered out of the room. As soon as he was gone, Indra hopped over two rows of seats and grabbed Cleo.

"C'mon," she said. She tossed Cleo in the air, then caught her. "Let's go before he gets you."

"You're helping me escape?" I asked, grabbing my knapsack.

"Let's just call it a field trip."

She waited till Mrs. Menendez left, and then peeked out the door.

"Coast is clear," she said, waving. "All the teachers have gone to lunch by now. And Nicky must be outside already."

"You know, maybe I should just get this over with." I looked up and down the hallway but saw no one. "If he doesn't get to pound on me today, he's going to be twice as mad tomorrow."

"Get this over with?" she repeated. "What are you going to do?" She thrust out her chin. "Say, 'Hey, Nicky, punch me right here'? Are you crazy? What kind of a plan is that?"

"It's the kind of plan you have when you have no plan. If not now, it'll be later. You know Dekker. He's responsible for so many bloody noses he attracts vampires."

Indra didn't answer. She just took my hand and dragged me from the class. That was nice—I mean, holding her hand, not being dragged, though I was afraid my palm was sweaty, seeing as I was about to have my head unscrewed. But Indra didn't say "Ewww" and wipe her hand or anything. She was pretty cool that way.

I heard something behind us.

I jerked Indra to a stop.

"Did you hear that?" I asked.

She nodded.

"What do you think? Maybe the monitors on their way to the schoolyard?" I suggested.

"Maybe."

Sure. If this were a monster movie, I would be the guy who always gets killed in the first five minutes.

We started walking again, this time on tiptoe.

Suddenly footsteps hammered behind us. Indra started to run, yanking me along with her. I looked over my shoulder and saw Dekker racing toward us.

"I got you now, Bertha!"

We skidded around a corner. Indra pointed to a door at the far end of the next, very long hallway.

"There!"

The door would lead us out onto the yard, which is what I had been trying to avoid in the first place. But I guess being pounded into dirt would be softer than being pounded into linoleum. I ran.

From behind I heard Dekker's voice, much too close.

"You'll never make it, Bertha!"

I was ready to let go of Indra's hand and to tell her to go ahead without me. Then I saw Cleo squeezed so tightly by Indra's fingers her mouth had been squished into an O. Plainly a call for help.

Okay. I would do it for Cleo.

With a blast of speed that would have shocked the gym teacher, I passed Indra, pulled her sharply to help her catch up, then exploded through the door. We had just collapsed (or at least *I* had collapsed) on the empty picnic table bench a few yards away, when we heard the door crash open behind us. A growling Dekker shot into the yard.

"Hel-looooo!" Indra suddenly began to wave. It reminded me of my mother helloing and waving yesterday in front of church, something I had been trying to forget.

"Sorry!" Indra called, still waving.

Had that last sprint cut off the oxygen to her brain?

"Sorry," she repeated loudly. "Won't run in the halls again."

I turned and looked. There stood four teachers, lined up along the wall as if being marched off to the principal's office, except the principal was among them.

"This is where they sneak out to smoke," Indra whispered. It was only then I saw the curls of gray streaming up from each one's hand. "I figured if you had to go out, there was no safer place."

Dekker saw the row of teachers. Even though they were slinking around the corner like the guilty culprits they were, he admitted temporary defeat. "Okay for now, but you can't hide forever, Bertha."

"I don't have to," I answered. "Just till Friday."

"No chance—not for you, not for *Cleo*. Isn't that what your *mommy* named her? Right before she asked about your brand-new recipe for Lemon Lace Wedding Cake? Whose was it again? Oh, that's right—Dolly Madison's. *Dolly*," he snorted.

I pressed the hidden chef's hat to my heart but couldn't defend myself.

"Didja hear that, Indra?" Dekker said into my silence. "Your wussy friend here just got a brand-new name—Baking Bertha."

"B-baking?" I said, not looking at Indra. "What do you mean 'Baking'?"

"I mean you're mommy's little cook. Do you wear her apron, too?"

"Nicky!" Indra scolded.

"*You* saw my mother," I said, clutching my knapsack. "She's a taco short of a combination plate."

"So what?"

"So, are you going to believe anything *she* says?" I asked, my face oven hot. "*Cook?* Even *I* think that's wussy."

At my double betrayal, it seemed that the sun dimmed and the earth shook. There before me, on one side, appeared the ghosts of famous chefs Jean Avice, Anton Careme, and George Auguste Escoffier. They shook their moldering French fists at me. On the other side stood the ghosts of their mothers, who rubbed their bony forefingers together. Shame on me! My denial tasted like ashes, like a mouthful of burnt toast.

And for what?

"Ha! Nothing's too wussy for you, Bertha," Dekker said, edging close. "*Baking* Bertha. I bet you've got cake plans for your little flour sack once the project's done. Give 'em up and say good-bye to Cleo now, Baking Bertha. It might be the last time you see her."

"You big bully," Indra said, stepping between us.

"Ooooh, I'm crushed," Dekker snapped, but a flash of something in his face said that maybe he was.

"Yeah, you're a bully, Nicky," Indra repeated, crossing her arms. Again a strange look flickered in his eyes, but she kept going. "After all this time, I've finally said it."

It was funny. I had always thought hurting Dekker could only be done with a return pounding. I never thought he could be affected by so simple a thing as a name. Maybe the name had to come from Indra to hurt.

Or maybe not.

"Yeah, you big bully," I echoed, giving my best attempt at a sneer. Stepping around Indra, Dekker snarled and made a fist.

"Bully, jerk, fat head." I frantically searched for the right word.

He tightened his fist.

"Jerk, slimeball, snot-face, turd."

He drew back his fist.

"Shrimp!" I blurted out. "Shorty!"

He threw the punch but it veered wildly and I was able to duck it. I, Bertie Hooks, had ducked a Dekker punch!

"Peanut! Ankle-biter!"

Embarrassment turned Dekker's face into a red-spotted mess. I felt myself puff up. Had it always been this easy?

He took a menacing step forward, but with a gulp, I stood firm and added, "Go away before somebody steps on you by mistake, you midget." I reached out and gave him a shove. He turned and, with hunched shoulders, walked back inside.

Indra punched me in the arm.

"That was so mean!" she said.

"What?" I couldn't believe her. "Like calling *me* 'Aunt Bertha' for years is nice? 'Good ol' Aunt Bertha,'" I said in a fair imitation of Dekker. "Now Baking Bertha. Or did you think I should just be used to it by now? Well, I'm not, Indra. I hate it!" I grabbed Cleo out of her hand. "And stop trying to save me all the time. I don't need your help!"

Indra followed Dekker inside.

Great. In a single morning, I had betrayed my mother, denied I liked to cook, managed to make my mortal enemy hate me even more, and probably just guaranteed I would never hold a girl's hand ever again.

I was going to fail eighth grade for sure now. Everyone hated me. My life was ruined. And it was only Monday.

DAY SEVEN, AFTERNOON

Late Tuesday afternoon, the intercom buzzed. Mrs. Menendez picked up the receiver and listened. "Yes, we're ready." She faced the class.

"Please, put your math books away," she said. She waited till the rustling and chair-scraping quieted. "Only three days remain till the end of the marking period this Friday," she continued. "Make-up homework from a few of you is still due, as well as some *special* projects." Her eyes narrowed and she looked back and forth between Dekker and me. "Other than that, our academic work for the year is finished. So over the coming days, I've arranged for a few guest speakers during my classes with you. Some parents have very generously interrupted their busy day to talk to you about their careers." She gestured toward the door as it started to open. "Please welcome our first guest, Mr. Peter Hooks."

Dad? My dad was giving up work to talk about work?

He hadn't said a word to me this morning on his way out the door. Maybe he had wanted to surprise me.

It was weird seeing him in class. It took me a few moments, then it hit me. I didn't *feel* weird, my father *looked* weird. He looked strange, unbalanced, not like my father at all. If I passed him on the street, I might not recognize him. Why?

"Mr. Hooks is, of course, Bertram Hooks's father," Mrs. M. said.

My father frowned when he saw Cleo on my desk. What was he thinking—that he had seen her face somewhere before, or that his newborn must be a genius to already be in eighth grade? He would be signing Cleo up for actuarial science, too.

Waving a hello to the class, he saw the second flour sack slumped on its side on Dekker's desk. My father did a double-take like from a Saturday morning cartoon. I could almost see the thought balloon over his head: *"Cleo has a twin?"*

"It's a class project, Dad," I tried to explain.

"And yours is named Cleo," Dekker cooed. "Soon to be Dolly."

"Shut up, Shorty," I answered.

Mrs. Menendez held up a warning finger to both of us. My father took that as his signal to start.

"Hi. I'm Peter Hooks, as you heard, Bert Hooks's father, and I would like to talk to you about insurance.

Most people think that insurance is boring, but it isn't, not at all. In most ways, it's all about protecting people and property, but on some levels, it's actually an exciting life-or-death gamble!"

My father's face glowed with enthusiasm, while mine glowed with embarrassment. I sank a little lower in my chair.

"Now my job is to figure out exactly what the chances are that any given accident, no matter how strange, might actually happen," he continued. "It may look like I'm only playing with numbers. But I'm really speculating about life; making up stories, even. It's a little like being a fiction writer and a little like being a detective, a detective of *future* events. Of course, I do have to translate all these strange tales into numbers, probabilities. So by the time I'm finished with the stories, rock star Head Cracker—"

The class gasped at the name and leaned forward eagerly.

"—becomes a statistic of .02379 percent in certain instances and 94.9 percent in others, depending on a whole set of variables, like whether he took his meds that day or whether the hotel maid gave Head Cracker ten pillows instead of his mandatory eleven pillows when she made up the room."

I heard murmurs of "Wow" and "How cool is that?" For *my* father?

"What's more, if you think about it," he said, "I also

contribute to either the decline of Western civilization or to the promotion of the arts, depending on your view of Head Cracker's music, since without his being insured to the gills, he wouldn't be allowed to play."

Beep-beep! At the sound, my father began to pat himself.

"And I, uh . . . can't even begin to tell you . . . um . . . about the consequences of a misplaced decimal," he said distractedly, patting first his shirt pockets, then his pant pockets.

Beep-beep!

His phone! My father was looking for his cell phone! No wonder I thought he had looked lopsided. I rarely saw that side of his head. When he checked in at the school office, he must have noticed the sign that read "No cell phones, no pagers, no beepers," thought it meant him, and turned his cell over to the secretary for safekeeping.

Now he wanted to answer the call of a digital watch.

As the guilty student fumbled to turn off the alarm, Mrs. Menendez glared. No beeps of any kind were allowed in class.

"Dad!" I waved my hand in the air to get his attention.

"Yes, son?"

"You can stop looking for your phone. That was a watch beeping."

"Oh," he said. He folded his hands in front of him. "Thank you. I guess I'm done, anyway. Questions anyone?"

Two dozen hands shot up, no doubt desperate to know more about Head Cracker. One voice jumped in without waiting.

"So, Mr. Hooks, your job is to pay up when freak accidents happen?" Dekker asked, his smile sneering and suspicious.

"Well, to help *determine* the chances that a payout will be neces—"

"So how much did you have to pay when your son was born?"

"Mr. Dekker," Mrs. M. said. "I'll remind you that Mr. Hooks is a parent."

"Oh, and that reminds me that *Mrs.* Hooks is a parent, too. I guess to get your son, you had to cross Mrs. Hooks with a—"

"Mr. Dekker, report to the principal's office at once!"

"What? What did I say?" He gave an exaggerated shrug.

She fixed him with a stare.

My father shifted uncomfortably from one foot to another.

"It's okay, Mrs. Menendez." He gave a nervous wave. "Really."

"No, Mr. Hooks. I have been unforgivably lax of late. As a result, the class has come to believe that the foolishness that goes on among themselves is acceptable elsewhere. It is not. I am so very sorry." She turned to Dekker. *"Go."*

For a very long moment, they stared at each other. Then Dekker stood up, shoved the flour bag off his desk, and stamped out of the room. The bag landed with an *oof* and a cloud of white dust.

Mrs. M. sat down.

"I apologize again, Mr. Hooks," she said. Her voice had a strange little hiccup to it. "Please, go on."

My father didn't answer, but only looked at her.

I raised my hand and waved it furiously.

"Dad! Dad!"

"Hmmm?" He turned to me.

"Dad, you said something about how important the decimal is."

He nodded.

"So why don't you tell us the story about the guy whose pen leaked? And there were decimal points everywhere?"

"That's right!" Relief made him look all rubbery. "That's a good one."

Instantly understanding, my father moved inch by inch to the left as he talked. This just happened to be farther and farther away from Mrs. M.'s desk at the right. When he had all the kids laughing, Mrs. Menendez took out a tissue and quietly blew her nose.

Despite the weakness betrayed by that soggy Kleenex, she recovered quickly. At the end of the story, she stood up, slam-dunked Dekker's flour sack into his knapsack, and picked up the bag. Then, in her sternest voice, she said, "Class, I'm escorting Mr. Hooks out. Not a word from any of you. Judy Boynton, you're in charge."

Mrs. M. and my father left. All of us stared at the open door.

For those last ten minutes, the class was perfect. No spitballs, no notes, not even whispers. Every so often, some frowning face would sneak a glance at me. No doubt people were wondering what Mrs. Menendez would say and do tomorrow, after today's disastrous parent visit.

Meanwhile, *I* was wondering how much Dekker's trip to the principal's office was going to cost me.

DAY SEVEN, NIGHT

 Sometimes, life is simple, and it's easy to figure people out. Are you a cat person or a dog person? Do you like deep-dish pizza or thin crust? Are you trustworthy, loyal, helpful, friendly, courteous, kind, obedient, cheerful, thrifty, brave, clean, and reverent—or Nick Dekker?

Almost as clear a division: Do you like your puttanesca sauce with anchovies or without?

Since I was making puttanesca for supper, the topic occurred naturally. Besides, it was easier and less stressful to think about cooking than about what had happened at school today. So I wondered, what is it about anchovies that is so divisive?

I minced the garlic that every recipe for puttanesca began with. Then I chopped up a good-sized onion, which was called for in some, though not all, recipes. But no one fought over onions.

When the garlic-onion mixture was sautéed nicely, I

stirred in both sun-dried and plum tomatoes. Many chefs used only plums. But no one fought over tomatoes.

Next, I threw in a half cup each of sliced green olives and sliced black olives. Some chefs insisted on only black olives in their puttanesca—Kalamata olives at that—yet no one really fought over olives.

But anchovies—that's where the line is drawn.

My father hated them. But anchovy-less puttanesca was a favorite of his, so it was no coincidence that I was making it tonight. I had a zillion questions to ask him when he came home from work.

What had happened after my father left class today? He had had to go back to the principal's office to get his cell phone. Did he get to hear Mrs. M. yell at Dekker? Was she going to suspend Dekker, maybe even expel him? And what about the rest of us? Had she said anything about there being consequences for the class? Did it involve terrible things like gym floors and toothbrushes?

And even these things were easier to wonder about than what the kids had thought of my dad today. Maybe that was the real reason I was making one of his favorite dishes. It was a guilt offering.

I pushed the thought away and measured out two tablespoons of capers, at last an ingredient that all recipes had in common. I tasted the puttanesca, adjusted the herbs, then put water on to boil for pasta. Fusilli, not spaghetti. The little curves hold the sauce better.

But all my chopping, slicing, and stirring were for nothing. My father didn't come home for dinner. He was working late, Mom explained, because of the time he had taken off that afternoon.

"I would have gone in his place, if Mrs. Menendez had only asked," Mom said. "Maybe she didn't think of it when we saw her on Sunday. Or maybe working in an insurance office is just more interesting than what I do. You know how some people are. It's the surface glamour that appeals to them."

Surface glamour? I almost choked on my fusilli, which, if you think about it, is pretty hard to do because it's so soft. Dad more interesting than Mom? Statistics more glamorous than astral projection? Good thing Mrs. M. *hadn't* asked her; Mom would have taught the kids bilocation. Then they could cut class without ever leaving the room.

"You know how much I love you, don't you, Bertie?" my mother asked without warning, staring down at her plate. Now I really *was* going to choke on my fusilli.

Was she a mind reader, too? Did she know how I had betrayed her yesterday in the schoolyard? Maybe her astral body *had* been there, hidden behind the angry French ghosts, hearing me deny both cooking and her. All of a sudden, my guilt about my father doubled and included her. When was my next appointment with Dr. Zimmerman?

"Uh, yeah," I said, starting to push my fusilli around.

"Well, um . . . uh, good," she said, imitating my movements. "What I mean is, you're very . . . very young, you know, and it's easy to make mistakes at that age, um . . . Ooops!" Some olives slid off her plate.

My ears must have been the color of the sauce.

"But sometimes we can catch our mistakes *before* we make them," my mother added hurriedly, wiping up the spill, still studying her plate. "And then everything's all right. Because the mistakes were never made. It's like erasing the past, except that particular past never happened, you see? It's almost like psychic time travel."

My embarrassment turned to confusion, which at least felt more familiar.

"Huh?"

She looked up at me and smiled widely. "I'm so relieved we had this little talk."

After dinner, I moped around for a bit, wondering about what she had said and why. Then I started thinking about Dekker's next attack. I had temporarily flustered him by calling him "Shorty" yesterday and again today in class. He got back at me through my father. But that backfired and Dekker had gotten in trouble, which meant his next attack would be direct. I had to take preventive action now.

It was eight o'clock. With the time difference between here and the West Coast, I just might catch someone still in the mill office. I brought Cleo to the living room and turned her bottom-side up. "Sorry," I whispered, hoping the blood didn't rush to her head, and then dialed the long-distance phone number stamped on her fanny.

"Granny Greta's Merry Mill," answered a man's gruff voice.

"Uh, hello? Can I talk to Granny Greta?"

"Who is this?"

"You don't know me. But I've got a sack of flour from back when you were Dutch's Old-Time Oregon Mill."

"This is a completely different company. I've told you bill collectors that a thousand times."

"I'm not a bill collector," I said. While I talked, I laid Cleo on a sofa pillow. "I thought maybe Granny Greta might know how to get in touch with Dutch. It's an emergency."

"That's what they all say."

"It really is," I tried to explain. "Please, I need to get an extra bag of Dutch's Old-Time Oregon Mill flour." Mrs. M. had said I couldn't do it, but I just had to try.

"You need a bag of flour?" asked the voice.

"Maybe two. It looks like it's going to be a very bad week. I'm expecting a terrible accident to happen at any minute."

"Accident? Are you getting wise with me? That warehouse fire was an accident. Is this the insurance company? Where's my money? I mean, Dutch's money?"

"What fire? No, don't tell me, I don't care," I said. "I just need a couple of sacks of flour, you know, the ones that read, 'Dutch's Old-Time Oregon Mill.'"

"Everything's in ashes. A complete tax write-off. Hey,

are you the IRS? I don't—I mean, Dutch doesn't owe you guys a dime. Or, well, that's what he told me before he left town."

"Dutch is gone?" It was the first part of this conversation I had understood. "Did he take all his flour bags with him?"

"There was nothing left to take. Listen up! I repeat: warehouse fire. It's toast. Got it? Crispy critters."

Instinctively I backed away from Cleo. Had she heard the loud voice over the receiver? She was the only one left. Did that make her an orphan? I had read about orphans in books, of course. It seemed you couldn't even be in a kid's book unless you were an orphan. But I had never known one myself.

"Do you have to shout?" I said. "So . . . there's nothing left?"

"Not a thing."

"Not even a few empty sacks?"

"Not a single one."

All at once I got an idea.

"You know how new businesses frame their first dollar bill?" I said. "Did Dutch frame his first sack of flour, just the bag? If he did, could you mail it to me overnight? Then it would all work out. I could put plain flour in it myself, see, and draw a face on it. Then I would have a fake Cleo to bring to school and when this terrible accident that's going to happen happens, the real Cleo will be safe."

"Cleo?"

"Yeah, Cleo, my flour-sack baby."

"You have a baby? And she's a flour sack?"

I sighed. "It's a *very* long story."

"You must think you're pretty clever, trying to convince me that you're crazy so I'll admit something. Well, it won't work."

"I'm not crazy. I'm just a desperate eighth grader. Please," I insisted. "Just let me talk to Granny Greta."

"This *is* Granny Greta. Now get lost, and take your flour-sack baby with you."

Click.

I shook my head. Granny Greta's Merry Mill needed better customer service.

As I hung up, I heard the front door open. I ran out into the hall and almost knocked my father down.

"Whoa!" he said, holding me back by the shoulders. "What's wrong, Bert?"

I felt all mushy inside, as if someone had tied me to a chair and made me watch *Bambi* three times in a row. I guess it was having my mother tell me she loved me. Or maybe it was hearing that Cleo was an orphan.

Suddenly I imagined one lonely little patch of white in a field of smoking ashes.

I was a traitor a dozen times over.

"Ready to talk yet, champ?"

I hated to be called that, especially when I knew I

would never make it to Friday. I pulled back and shoved my hands in my pockets.

"What's going on?" my father asked.

"Nothing."

"Really?" He ducked his head till it was level with mine. "Your mother thinks you're going to run away. Bertie, that would break your mother's heart. Mine, too."

"What?" Is that why she had told me she loved me, and what she meant about making mistakes at my age? "What do you mean, 'run away'?"

"Well, that's what you intend to do, isn't it? Run away and become a spy?"

"A spy?"

"I had such different plans for you, son. I really wanted you to join me at the company. But a . . . a . . . "

"A spy?" I repeated, still not believing what I had heard. This was too weird, even for *my* family.

"It's okay," my father said. "Your mother told me all about the letter. She called at the office this afternoon."

"Letter? What letter?" My heart started to thump a bit quicker.

"The letter from the CIA. Bert, that kind of life is so dangerous, no insurance company in the world would give you a policy!"

The letter! The letter that for months I had been waiting for, dying for, praying for. The letter I had pushed out of my mind entirely just so I wouldn't spend every second of every minute of every hour thinking about it—*the letter from the CIA!*

I ran up to my parents' bedroom.

"Mo-o-o-om!"

I found her sitting cross-legged on the bed, half a dozen books opened before her.

"Where is it?" I demanded.

"Oh, honey, why? And why did they have to answer you through the regular mail?" she asked. "Just getting a *letter* from the CIA could put you in danger. There could be counterspies everywhere!"

"Where is it? Where is it?"

She slid her hand under her pillow and pulled out a business-size envelope.

I snatched it, ran into my room, and slammed the door behind me. For long minutes, I was afraid to do more than stare at the return address—CIA, the Culinary Institute of America.

The Culinary Institute. How had I dared to even write the school, much less apply there? Me—traitorous Bertie Hooks, who hadn't even told my own parents I wanted to be a chef? I didn't deserve to get in. I didn't deserve to wear white.

I opened the envelope. The CIA agreed.

"Application denied."

DAY EIGHT

 "You have Dr. Zimmerman after school," my mother said, pouring a bowl of cereal. "I'm skipping yoga and will come pick you up after class."

"Dr. Zimmerman? I didn't know I had him on a Wednesday."

"I saw him yesterday. Yesterday before I . . . got home."

Yesterday before I got the mail, her face said, full of motherly hints. I refused to talk about the letter from the CIA.

"He was very eager that you come in, Bertie, something about your being on the verge of a breakthrough."

Breakdown was more like it. Yesterday's rejection had topped it off, though I tried to tell myself things weren't too bad. Once I pulled my eyes from that horrible word "denied," I found out I was being turned down because I was too young. While my application had been exemplary, they said, applicants to the Culinary Institute had to be high school graduates. They also needed six months of kitchen experience in a "non-fast-food environment," plus a letter of recommendation from an industry professional. Cooking at home didn't count.

I had been so sure I'd get in. My application essay was about my goal of being a Certified Master Chef. There were only a few dozen CMCs in the whole country, which made sense, since the exam alone took ten days. Plus, even though original recipes weren't required, I had included my best: Death by Eggplant. The dish was a cross between baba ghanouj and eggplant parmigiana, with a few twists of my own. A single spoonful of it could bring tears to my eyes and banish any doubts I had about my abilities as a chef. And the admissions committee tried it! I knew because there had been a telltale smudge of garlic on the letter.

With all this, admitting me should have been a no-brainer. Never mind the nice words about looking forward to hearing from me in four more years. If this were France, I would already be packing my bag. But it wasn't France. I needed a high school diploma, which meant I first needed to pass eighth grade.

Sighing, I set a bowl of Oatie-O's and milk in front of Cleo. She had no teeth, but the cereal would get mushy enough if I let it sit. While I did this, part of me was saying, "How silly, flour sacks don't eat." Another part said that if I didn't feed Cleo *something*, she would get cranky by gym. When Mrs. M. found out why, family services would be called in, and I would be found guilty of flour-sack abuse. Not the path to a passing grade.

I began to pack my knapsack. Last night, I erased all the marks in my books so I could turn them in.

"When you pick me up after school, why don't you wait around back," I suggested to my mother. "Less traffic." And less of a crowd to see her in a turban.

"Okay," she said. "Three o'clock, around back, then off to Dr. Zimmerman. Maybe . . . maybe you'll talk to *him* about . . . "

"See you later, Mom," I said quickly.

Indra was waiting for me on my porch.

"I'm still mad at you for calling Nicky 'Shorty' and shoving him," she said at once, playing with the end of her braid. Then she dropped it and looked up. "But I'm so furious with Nicky. I couldn't believe how mean he was to your father yesterday."

And I couldn't believe Indra Sahir had come over this early just to tell me that. Maybe my life wasn't ruined after all.

Hiding my grin, I jumped from the porch and ran to the sidewalk.

"Where's the baby?" Indra called.

"In my knapsack."

"Isn't that stuffy?"

"It's better than sunburn," I answered.

"Oh." She hurried after me for a while, then gave up. "Bertie, stop running! We've got plenty of time." She stood still, hands on her hips. I slowed down, then slowed even more. She caught up.

When she was at my side, she said, "Oops, your books are falling out." She walked in back of me and fussed with my knapsack. I held my breath, waiting to hear the zip of the inner pocket being opened.

"I really liked your father yesterday," Indra said. "He was pretty cool."

"*My* father? *Cool?*" Had she been in the same class as me yesterday?

"Yeah, all that stuff he said about weird stories and taking chances on whether or not they'll happen. And working with people like Head Cracker. His job sounded sooo interesting."

I shrugged. "Maybe. He never really explained it like that before," I admitted.

"And I really liked what *you* did yesterday. But I'm not surprised. I always knew you were nice," she said from behind me.

My father was "cool." *I* was "nice." I had used the same word thanking my Great Aunt Ethel for my birthday socks.

"What do you mean, 'nice'?" I asked. Maybe details would help.

"You know, nice for you and your father to distract the

kids. So they wouldn't look at Mrs. Menendez while she was upset."

"While she was crying," I corrected.

"You are *so* wrong! Mrs. M. was *not* crying!" Indra yanked my knapsack zipper shut. "She was just emotional. It made her nose run."

My score on the nice-meter was dropping.

"If *I* got that emotional, I'd never hear the end of it," I said. "'Cry-baby.' 'Sissy boy.' 'Weepy peepy.'"

"Weepy peepy?"

I shrugged. "It's a family expression."

"Weepy peepy?"

"Because my nose squeaks when I cry, all right? I mean, cried. When I was little. Real little."

"Squeaks?"

"A little peeping noise, according to my mother. I'd cry and squeak, then she'd say, 'Weepy peepy' and get me to laugh."

"That is *sooo* cute, Bertie."

I turned on her. "If you ever tell Dekker, I swear I'll–"

She put a finger on my mouth. It was supposed to shush me. It nearly stopped my heart.

"Your secret's safe," she said.

"Is it?" I started to walk, just to get my heart pumping again. "Now you tell *me* a secret. So I'll know I can trust you." Then maybe, I thought, maybe I would tell her a *real* secret. Fixing my books, she had been inches from the chef's hat hidden in my knapsack. And I realized that, even though I had held my breath, I hadn't been afraid. I almost wanted her to discover it.

"All right, a secret," she said. "But not a word to anyone, promise?" Braid flying, she quickly looked over her shoulder, then back at me. She lowered her voice. "I'm engaged."

"What?!"

"Shhhh! Since I was six and my fiancé was one. *One!* I was engaged to a baby!" She clapped her hands over her giggle. "He's eight now. He's getting older. That's not good."

"Where is this guy?"

"He's in India. My mother arranged it. She is so old-fashioned. She still wears a bindhi—you know, that colored dot on her forehead—plus she dresses in a sari. And not just on holidays. She's a blood-work technician, and she wears a sari to the lab. She wears a sari just to get pizza! It is *so* embarrassing to be seen with her."

"My mother wears a sari, too, sometimes," I offered. "It *is* embarrassing. What does your father say?"

"I can go to college here, while we wait for my fiancé to grow up. Then it's back to India. How can they do this to me?" She kicked at a stone in her path. "If I have kids, I will never, ever, *ever* be this mean to them."

"Maybe it's not that bad," I suggested.

Indra looked at me as if I had grown horns.

"You don't have to worry about who likes you or not," I explained. "Hey, you don't even have to worry about having a date for the senior prom."

Indra was about to explode, but then kids from another grade crossed the street right in front of us. Though her face was twelve shades of purple, she poked me to be quiet.

At the classroom door, Dekker shoved past me, muttering, "Move it, Bertha," then sat down. He pulled his flour sack out and dropped it on the floor. The sack bore a smudge, as if he had managed to kick it without splitting open the paper. At my own desk, I turned Cleo to face me, so she wouldn't be frightened by the bruise.

For a few moments, I fantasized that Mrs. M. wouldn't show up, Mrs. M. who supposedly hadn't missed a day in, like, a hundred and thirty-eight years. I imagined that she had fled the country, or maybe even was in a loony bin for cracked-up teachers. Dekker had broken her yesterday. Dekker had made her cry.

But no, she was right on time for homeroom and was her usual brisk self, which made me think that maybe Indra had been right and yesterday's tissue was only for a runny nose.

When we went back to Spanish right before lunch, we found another guest parent waiting, a short man with Brillo-pad eyebrows, a huge clown smile, and such a strong accent he needed dubbing. I missed his name. Then I saw

Juliska Lovass-Nagy sitting so low in her desk all I could see was the part in her hair. Just another victim of embarrassing parents.

Both in homeroom and now, before and after Mr. Lovass-Nagy's visit, Mrs. M. never said a word about yesterday or about "special consequences." It was as if it had never happened. She also never said a word to Dekker about his dirty flour sack. She stared at the smudge, stared at Dekker, stared back at the smudge, and made a note in her book. Then she looked at Cleo and me and walked to the back of the class to my seat.

I had always hated throwing out pencil stubs. It seemed such a waste, even when they were too itty-bitty for my fingers. Now at last I had a use for them. They were the perfect flour-sack-baby size. So I had sharpened a bunch of two-inch stubs and lined them up in front of Cleo. I had even given her my homework pad. Mrs. Menendez looked at us, Cleo and me, little pencils and big pencils, little pad and big pad.

"Your enthusiasm makes things rather crowded, Mr. Hooks."

"You're right," I agreed. "I know it's very late in the year, but do you think Cleo could get her own desk? I'm a righty and she's a lefty and we keep banging elbows."

Mrs. M. didn't answer. She simply made another note in her book and returned to the front of the room.

When school was finally over, I tucked Cleo into my

knapsack, ran out the back door, and hopped into the waiting car.

My mother must have rushed out at the last minute to get me, because she wasn't dressed up in her usual scarves, fringes, and turban. Instead, she wore plain leggings and a T-shirt that read "Having an out-of-body experience. Back in ten minutes." It was supposed to be a joke, but sometimes I wondered if Mom was trying to give the rest of the world an actual warning.

"There's a snack for you in the bag," she said, pointing. This was almost as much of a shock as her making me lunch. I pulled out a juice box and a granola bar for myself and a cracker for Cleo. I strapped Cleo into the car seat, stuck the cracker in between the seat belt and her drawn-on face, then settled down and buckled myself in.

After a long silence, my mother said, "It's Cleo, isn't it? I think you've been visualizing much too hard, Bertie. You've projected genuine feelings onto your school project, feelings you really shouldn't be feeling, like jealousy. That's why you want to run away and become a spy, isn't it?"

"I'm not going to become a spy, Mom," I said. "Really, I'm not."

"Well, what about the letter, Bertie? Or are you going to tell me there's no letter, either?"

I looked out the window. The drive to the doctor's office was taking forever.

"There was a letter," I admitted.

"And what does 'CIA' stand for, if not the 'Cruel Interruption of Affection' between a mother and her son?"

This was my chance. Could I say it?

"'CIA' stands for the 'Culinary Institute of America,' Mom." I swallowed. My throat was dry. "The letter was from the Culinary Institute of America. I want to *go* to the Culinary Institute of America."

"Culinary? That has to do with food, right?"

"Right," I said, sagging with relief.

"You want to be a *farmer*?"

There was a sharp crack, the sound of my hopes breaking.

I felt as if I had dared everything, put the deepest, most meaningful part of my life out there for her, and she had completely misunderstood. It had taken everything I had to say "Culinary Institute of America." I couldn't talk about it anymore.

"Look, a parking spot!" I pointed, glad to be at Dr. Zimmerman's. When my mother stopped the car, I unbuckled Cleo, tucked her under my arm, and ran up to the office.

Dr. Zimmerman beamed as he opened the door. "So, so, so," he said happily. The pointy ends of his mustache almost twirled on their own. Then he saw Cleo, and the mustache tips drooped. "*Sooo.* I see we have regressed since Saturday." He shook his head. "I knew it was too much too soon. Come in, and tell me why you have done this thing."

"Done what?" I said, sitting down and balancing Cleo on my knee.

"Made this, this *dummy* as a substitute for your sister, no?"

"No, this is my sister. I mean, this is what Cleo has always been. I thought that once you saw her, you'd understand."

His eyebrows lifted with an idea. "Do you pinch this little flour bag? Poke it? Punch it?"

I thought of the bruise on Dekker's bag. "Of course not! Does she look like she's been punched?"

He leaned over and pointed. On Cleo's head was a Band-Aid, which I had put on her tear to replace the tape.

"What is this, then, that you did to her?"

"This isn't a her, this is a flour sack!"

"True, but in the moist and murky mud of your subconscious, this *is* your little sister. Don't you see how you're regressing? First, you would bake her into cupcakes and serve her as a ritual meal to your mother. Now your hostility has snowballed into explicit violence."

"What does that mean?" I asked.

"It means you may want to hurt Cleo."

"Never!" I pulled Cleo closer. "I shouldn't have brought her here."

"Then why did you?" he asked, steepling his fingers.

"I don't know. So you'd see. Plus, I think you're confusing my mother. She's way too deep into this project."

"Ah, *your mother*." The doctor put the box of tissues in front of me. "So, Bertram, what about your mother? What do you want to tell me?"

The words tumbled out: "How can a woman who knows Middle English and hieroglyphics not know the word 'culinary'?"

"Hmm?" His eyebrows rose.

"This is a flour sack," I said. "My mother can remember to bring it a cracker and can run out and buy it a baby car seat, but she can't recognize when I tell her *the most important thing in my life!*"

"Are you asking your mother to make a choice?" Dr. Zimmerman's eyebrows shot up so far they disappeared into his hair.

"There *is* no choice. I mean, how can there be?"

"You sound worried. Don't you think she will choose you?"

"I don't know—*Yes!*" I said quickly, then weakened, "but . . . "

"But what?" he asked, his voice suddenly gentle. "You can say it, Bertram. You can say anything here."

"It's just that a flour sack may be . . . less disappointing than a real kid. Cleo isn't getting beat up by bullies because she can't stand up for herself. Of course, she can't stand up at all, but you know what I mean." My brief victory over Dekker evaporated. All I could remember were the years of being pounded. "And Cleo isn't going to shock anyone by failing math, though I did try to explain I was having trouble. No one seemed to hear me."

Dr. Zimmerman nodded over and over.

"You cry for help, but no one listens, no?"

"Yes. I mean, no, no one listens. And Cleo is really small and cute and cuddly, while I'm . . . "

"Yes?"

"I'm . . . I'm me."

"Yes, yes, a very serious fault," he agreed, still nodding. "I can see now why your mother might have difficulty choosing."

"What?" I sat up straight. "You're supposed to be on *my* side."

"Why should I be? Cleo sounds so much more likable, capable even, for one so young."

"I'm capable!"

"Of what?" He pointed at Cleo's face. "Even your artwork is lacking."

"I don't have to be an artist. I . . . I can cook," I said, my face burning. "I love to cook." How strange, how wonderful the words felt!

"You mean, it's easier to take home economics than a harder math course. Cooking, there's no future in it," Dr. Zimmerman said.

"No future?" I yelled. "Tell that to Emeril, Jacques Pépin, Wolfgang Puck—"

"*Pffft.*"

"–Todd English, Masaharu Morimata, and, and–What if somebody way back had told that to *James Beard*?" My voice dropped reverently and I said, "Father of American cooking."

"Double *pfffft*." The doctor shrugged to dismiss me. "You mean, you will be saying, 'Would you like fries with that?'"

"This is exactly why I don't tell anyone!" I said, jumping to my feet. "I'm going to be a great chef! I'm going to go to the Culinary Institute of America. I'm going to have a prime-time cooking show, and a four-star restaurant, and a best-selling cookbook. I'm also going to have a bed-and-breakfast to fall back on, because I know you shouldn't put all your eggs in one basket!"

I collapsed into my chair, panting. I had never said so much about cooking out loud before, and certainly not with so many "I's" stuck in.

"So much ambition, so much passion," Dr. Zimmerman said softly. "*Tch, tch,* who would have suspected it? Your mother thinks you're going to be a famous psychoanalyst."

"What? When did she say this?"

"Our last session. Something about your being a master of dream interpretation. Who else interprets dreams but psychoanalysts?" The doctor's eyebrows rose. "So, you would take *my* job, too, yes?"

"I don't want your job. I'm going to be a chef!"

"I should believe this of a boy who's failing math? No, no, no."

"Yes, yes, yes!" How had this gotten so far from whether I had a sister or a flour sack? "It makes perfect sense. I'm too busy cooking to waste time on algebra homework."

"But a chef? A restaurant owner? A television star? *Pffft,"* said Dr. Zimmerman, leaning back. "These hopes are so much in the future. You will be old then. Cleo, too, will be old and able to take care of herself. It is *now* that you cannot deal with her, *now* that you concoct all these fantasies." He stroked the tip of his beard. "Tell me, Bertram Hooks, what is your heart's desire *right now*? What do you really and truly want *this very minute* from all the people around you?"

"I want my mother to remember she's my mother. I want my father to accept me for who I am. I want Nick Dekker to be kidnapped by aliens. I want Indra Sahir to kiss me. And I want Mrs. M. to promote me to ninth grade."

"Mmm," the doctor said. "And Cleo?"

"I don't want anything from Cleo. She can't give me anything."

"She can love you, Bertram. And maybe, because it isn't complicated with these other problems, maybe hers is the clearest, truest love."

Sighing, I turned Cleo's sweet cross-eyed face toward mine.

"Maybe you're right."

DAY NINE

 "It's Thursday," I said, talking to my sleepy-eyed face in the bathroom mirror. "Just today and tomorrow left. You can do it!"

Gee, that sounded convincing. And if I couldn't believe in myself, how were other people supposed to take me seriously?

I needed to be older. Then when I explained my dreams—no, my *goals*—people would listen. They wouldn't stroke their beards and say, *"Pfffft!"*

A beard.

I squirted foam from my father's can of shaving cream and made myself a full white beard. It looked pretty good. In fact, it made me look like a recent competitor on *Iron Chef,* my favorite program. I loved everything about the Japanese TV show, down to the bad dubbing that made the episodes seem like a cross between *Godzilla,* the WWF, and Julia Child. But the Japanese understood. It was all about mastering the food.

I growled at my bearded reflection in the bathroom mirror.

"Arrrh! Iron Chef French—you are going *down*! Aarrrrh, arrrrrh!"

Plain white toques weren't dramatic enough for TV, so many of the competitors wore colorful costumes. I wrapped a long red bath towel around my shoulders as a cape and a smaller red hand towel straight up around my head like a chef's hat. That was better.

I pointed to my chest. "Iron Chef Italian takes no prisoners!"

I didn't really have enough specialties to claim a country. But I had already made puttanesca sauce this week and planned risotto for dinner. So today I would be Italian. Maybe I should add being Iron Chef to my list of goals. "Arrrh!" Now when I spoke to my reflection, I believed it. "Just today and tomorrow left. You can do it! *Aarrrh!!*"

"Do what, Bert?" My father stopped at the open door.

I yanked the hand towel off my head and wiped my face, all in one movement.

"Survive the week," I said, knocked back to being plain old Bertie Hooks.

"Survive? What do you mean, champ?" Dad asked, punching a number into his phone.

Maybe I had finally been brain damaged by secondhand cell-phone radiation. Or maybe I was just embarrassed, having been caught growling at myself while wearing a red cape and a shaving-cream beard.

"I'm not your champ!" I snapped at my father's reflection.

"Hi, no, wait a minute," he said into the phone. He held it down at his side. "Are you okay?"

"What if I said no?"

Without another word, he ended the call.

"What's wrong?" he asked.

Where should I begin? Last week, when he let Mom become mother to a flour-sack baby? Years ago, when he let the office become more important than his family? Or how about when I was first born and he let me be named "Beorhthramm" instead of "John?"

His cell phone rang, probably the person he had just called calling him back. This was my chance, my maybe once-in-a-lifetime opportunity to spill everything.

"Bert?"

But would he really listen to me? And what would he say?

The repeated chirp of the phone made me twitch.

"Answer it!" I yelled.

He switched the phone off entirely.

"Not until you answer me. What's wrong?"

Quickly I rinsed my face.

"It's okay," I told him.

He said nothing.

"Really," I insisted, then added, "For now anyway."

"And then what?"

"I'll explain things," I said. "Just not now."

"You promise?"

I nodded.

"You know," he said, leaning against the doorjamb, "all this talk about your running away to be a spy . . . it's brought back such memories."

"Memories? *You* were a spy?"

"Oh, no no no, there's not much of a retirement package for spies, now is there? I mean, memories of when you were a baby, all the plans I had for you." My dad smiled, and his eyes got a misty far-off look. "I remember every minute of the day you were born. Your mother phoned my office at 11:37 in the morning, and I said I'd race right over. By 12:03 I got her to the hospital, and at 7:14 that night you were born. When I saw you, the first thing I said was, 'That boy has the hands of an actuary.' So you can see, this spy business has caught us all by surprise."

I looked down at my hands. The streaks of shaving foam looked like whipped cream.

"Well, I guess accounting could come in handy," I admitted, "say, if I were . . . doing the books of a restaurant."

"A restaurant?" my father said. "Oh, we'll have much bigger clients than that to insure. Mega-multi corporations with branches around the world. You and me, champ."

Hints were not going to work with my parents. Maybe if I went on a cooking strike and forced them to eat canned soup every night, they would finally notice what I had been doing all these years.

Canned soup?

During my last cold, my mother had tucked me into bed, put a box of tissues near me, and said, "I'll make you some nice hot chicken soup, Bertie." Smiling, I settled in for a long nap. But she was back just five minutes later, carrying a bowl of thin yellow liquid. Canned soup. Microwaved. I hadn't even known the stuff was in the house.

Coughing and sniffling, I dragged myself downstairs and opened the freezer door. Out came the chicken wings and necks I always kept on hand to make stock. Out came the onions and celery, carrots and parsley. Out came the pot. I sliced the onions—under cold running water to keep from crying. The circles within circles, white on white, led me into a zenlike calm. And when I chopped rib after rib of celery, each little half moon seemed to smile at me. *That* was what was missing from canned soup, besides the taste—that incredible energy, the relationship that flowed from cook to food to guest (or, in this case, from cook to food and back to cook again). Assembly-line soup had no heart in it; it could nourish the body, but not the soul.

But my parents didn't get this. Canned soup didn't bother them.

As I trudged to school, the words "Just today and tomorrow, today and tomorrow" pounded in my head like a march. But the closer to school I got, the less likely my living till tomorrow seemed. Tomorrow I only needed to show up and let Mrs. M. see my near-perfect flour sack. Dekker wouldn't try anything then, not after Mrs. Menendez had seen Cleo. So today would be his last chance, and that meant all-out war.

"I'm in danger, Bertie!" I could almost hear the whisper from my knapsack. "Don't let anything happen to me."

"I'll keep you safe," I whispered back, before I knew what I was doing. I spent the rest of the walk to school making sure I didn't talk to my flour sack.

In class, half the kids had that jiggly "Summer's here, let me *out!*" itch, while the other half had mid-June sleepies. Foot tapping competed with snores. Indra put her head down on her desk. I watched as she carefully arranged her long loose hair across her face like a curtain to block out the sun. Even triple A+ Judy Boynton was staring open-mouthed out the window at the sunny day.

Mrs. M. took the homeroom roll. All the flesh-and-blood students were present. Both flour-sack students were present. We were ending the year with a full house.

The day continued lazily through the afternoon, with most of the teachers as summer-struck as we were. By last-period math, most of the kids were reading comics or books they had brought from home. Cleo was watching me use her memo pad to make tiny paper airplanes.

The intercom buzzed. Mrs. M. picked up the receiver and listened.

"Oh," she said into the intercom. "No, there's no problem. It's just unfortunate timing. I meant to cancel, then forgot."

Mrs. M. forgot something? The shock registered on the Richter scale.

"No, don't say anything," she said into the receiver. "Just send her in."

Send *her* in?

This could be bad, very bad. I could already hear my mother telling about the time she painted hieroglyphics on our roof in glow-in-the-dark paint.

A moment later, there was a knock. Mrs. Menendez opened the door, and I tensed up, prepared to hurl myself out the classroom window.

In walked the fattest woman I had ever seen. She was short, too, so she was like a ball walking into the room. I expected her to roll.

"Look out!" someone whispered. "Free Willy escaped her tank."

The woman wore a black jacket, black slacks, a black-and-white dotted vest, and a frilly white blouse beneath. There was no way to escape the image of a killer whale.

"Hello, Mrs. Menendez!" she said right away, reaching

out and pumping Mrs. M.'s hand. Then she waved. "Hi, Nicky! Surprise!"

Surprise? How about catatonic shock?

"Hi, everyone!" she called. "I'm Mrs. Dekker, Nicky's mom."

Most of the class mumbled a stunned "Hi," though Jerome Lindsay next to me said, "Gee, Dekker, you're lucky she didn't squash you giving birth." Dekker turned. He stared at *me*, his face as mean and scary as it had ever been. There was no point in saying I wasn't the one making the wisecracks. I had *seen* his mother. That was enough.

Now I knew why he had been holding cans of diet drinks when I ran into him in the supermarket.

And now I knew why Mrs. Menendez had meant to cancel. After the fiasco with my father, having Dekker's mother in to talk was weird and awkward. What I didn't understand was how Mrs. M. could have forgotten.

"Mrs. Dekker is a lawyer, class," Mrs. Menendez said, as mildly as if I should not be out this very second getting measured for my coffin. "You may have heard about the student who recently sued her teacher, her school, and her school district. The student claimed that assigning homework and penalizing her for not doing it was an invasion of her privacy. Her lawyer said it was similar to a company trying to restrict what an employee does in his or her personal life. That made homework and penalties for not doing it a violation of her Fourteenth Amendment rights. Mrs. Dekker successfully defended *against* the claim, and the student lost."

Kids started to groan. Right away, Mrs. Dekker waved both hands no and stepped up to speak.

"Ladies and gentlemen of the jury," she began. "I can see that you're already prejudiced. But I ask you to put your own feelings aside and keep an open mind as I present my case."

In fifteen minutes, that woman had us convinced that homework was not only legal, it was the moral and cultural base upon which the whole world's civilization rested. She was so good I forgot I hated homework. I forgot she was fat. I even forgot she was Dekker's mother. When she asked for questions, my hand was first in the air.

The class gasped. I yanked my hand back down, but it was too late.

"You in the back." Mrs. Dekker tilted her head to get a better look, then broke into a laugh. "Oh, another flour sack!" she said. "Mrs. Menendez did say another boy had the 'same challenge' as Nicky. How's it going?"

"Fine, ma'am, thank you."

"Your question?"

"I, uh, oh, I forgot," I blurted out. For some reason, the class laughed.

Smiling, Mrs. Dekker shook her head and *tsk-tsk*ed. "You'd make a very bad witness," she said.

"Yes, I know, I mean, actually I wouldn't know—because I'd forget. I can't remember anything. For example, I won't remember you were ever here. In fact, I've already forgotten." I wiped my damp palms on my pants. "Did I just say something?"

This time the laughter was unreasonably long and unreasonably hard.

"What do you think?" Mrs. Dekker turned to Mrs. M. "Should I mark him as a hostile witness?"

"I'm not hostile!" I protested in alarm, glancing at Dekker. He was facing front, his jaw clenched so tight I could practically count his teeth through his cheeks. "I like you, I really do."

"It just means you're uncooperative," Mrs. Dekker said.

"I'll cooperate, please. Just tell me what you want. If you want me to testify, I'll testify. If you want me to love homework, I'll love homework. Heck, I'll even *do* homework."

"This smells of bribery. Do homework in return for what?" Mrs. Dekker asked.

"Uh, live through the day?"

She frowned. " 'Live through the day'? Have you been threatened? Are you suggesting that you need the witness protection program?"

Yes, against your son—the words danced in my mouth, frantic to get out. I choked them back.

"No, no threats, not from no one, no one at all," I finally managed to say.

"Well then, I have a question for *you*." Mrs. Dekker narrowed her eyes as she looked at me. "Why is your flour sack wearing a baby hat?"

"To protect her from drafts."

"Oh. Uh, thank you, that's all. Any other questions?"

"Yeah," said Jerome Lindsay. "How did you get so fat?"

"Eating too many bratty kids. They make me bloat."

Dekker jumped up and flew out the door.

"Let him go," Mrs. Dekker said to Mrs. M. She turned back to the class. "Any legitimate questions?"

Mrs. Dekker was as cool as a cucumber. I bet she could be defending a guy for murder, have him break down in the witness chair and confess in a crowded courtroom, and she would change tactics without a blink—and win.

"No, that's enough questions," said Mrs. Menendez. "Mr. Lindsay, apologize to Mrs. Dekker, then take yourself down to the principal's office."

Jerome pulled himself to his feet, mumbled an apology, then left the room. Mrs. M. whispered her own apology, which Mrs. Dekker waved off. The two walked out into the hall. Mrs. M. returned for a second. "I want a five-hundred-word essay from the lot of you on the meaning of courtesy. Start now. Finish it up for homework. Miss Boynton, hand out paper from my desk to anyone who needs it. Mr. Hooks, come with me to the office, please."

Stunned, I trailed behind them to the principal's office.

Why did I have to go with them? What had *I* done? It wasn't fair.

When the three of us reached the office, Mrs. M. asked Mrs. Dekker if she knew about Tuesday's incident with my father. No, Mrs. Dekker didn't. She had been away on business and apparently neither her husband nor her son had shared that bit of news on her return. So Mrs. M. summed it up, then explained how Dekker might have mis-interpreted both his mother's presence here today and any comment I had made. Skating around the really important points, Mrs. M. never mentioned that my family was loony or that Mrs. Dekker's son was rotten. The bell rang, and Mrs. M. kept talking.

Finally there were apologies all around, from Mrs. M. for letting the class get so out of control, from me for not keeping my mouth shut, from Mrs. Dekker for not know-ing her son had been causing problems in school. It was a real lovefest. Any minute, I thought we were going to exchange friendship bracelets.

"Don't let me keep you, Mr. Hooks," Mrs. M. said to me.

"Yeah, I've got that long, *long* essay to write, too."

This was Mrs. M.'s chance to say, "Why, of course that didn't apply to *you*, Mr. Hooks. After all, you're the poor victim in this dreadful mess."

Instead she said, "Five hundred words. And I *will* count. One day you'll thank me, Mr. Hooks. You can go now."

Since it was so late, I could leave the building straight from the office. That's when I realized that I didn't have my knapsack with me. I had been so shocked about going to the principal's office that I had left my knapsack in the classroom.

My knapsack! My toque!

The class was empty by the time I ran down the hall and burst into the room. The bus kids, after-school-care kids, even walkers like Indra had all left. But there was my knapsack, just where I left it. I grabbed it up, unzipped the inner pocket, and stuck in my hand. The feel of cotton was smooth, cool, and comforting.

Relieved, I scooped up the pens and paper on my desk in one hand and went to grab Cleo with the other.

Cleo was gone.

And on the floor beside my foot, as ghastly as a smear of blood, was a smudge of flour.

DAY TEN

It was three A.M. I had spent five sleepless hours tossing in bed. I was a wreck.

Over and over, I kept thinking, what can I do? What can I possibly do?

Absolutely nothing.

I had failed the assignment. Now I would have to go to summer school, maybe even repeat eighth grade. My own class would be gone, and I would be left alone to tower over shrimpy seventh graders. Worse, my having to repeat a grade would look horrible when I reapplied to the Culinary Institute.

Worser—Indra would be gone, too, over to the high school across town. No way would she want to be seen with someone from junior high, even though I was older than her fiancé.

At last I fell asleep. The worrying became a dream with a very sarcastic voice.

"Oh, boo hoo," it said. "Poor Bertie might have to go to summer *school. What about poor Cleo? Have you given a second's thought to her? Her life is in danger!"*

"She's a flour sack," I answered.

"She's your baby!"

Cleo appeared. *"I'm your baby!"* she pleaded. She started to grow little arms and legs. Then Cleo turned into Chuckie, the demon doll from all those horror videos I never should have watched.

"Ah ha!" Cleo/Chuckie crowed. "I'm the child of lies!"

Suddenly I was in school, running down an endless hallway, as Cleo/Chuckie chased me with a knife. A door appeared. I rushed through it into a huge kitchen. I began to throw egg grenades. From nowhere, I grabbed a hose and milk spurted out. The powdery white legs became sticky. Cleo/Chuckie got stuck to the floor and couldn't move. I had just turned on the electric beater when Cleo/Chuckie became Cleo again.

"Save me," she whispered. "Be brave, Chef Bertie, and save me . . . "

She melted into a puddle of white goo, wailing pitifully, "Save me, save me!"

I woke up, heart pounding, body sweating. I rushed to my parents' bedroom.

"Mom! Dad! Help!"

My mother popped straight up.

My father, snoring loudly, lay sprawled on his stomach. His hand was stretched toward the floor, where his cell phone, calculator, pen, sheets of paper, and a book light, still on, were scattered.

"Dad!" I grabbed the big toe that stuck out beneath the sheet and shook hard. "Wake up, Dad!"

"Sixty-two one hundredths, and not a point more," he mumbled.

"Mom, Dad! It's Cleo!"

"What?" they asked, both waking up.

"Remember last night when you asked where Cleo was and I told you she was at a sleepover at Patty Cakes?" I took a deep breath. "Well, I lied. Cleo's been kidnapped."

"Kidnapped?!" they shrieked in unison. Two of my mother's curlers popped—*sproing!*—right off her head.

"At first I didn't care, and I wasn't going to do anything about it," I confessed. "I mean, she's just a flour sack and this whole thing has gotten way out of hand, and so what if I have to go to summer school or even repeat eighth grade? I do *not* want a flour sack for a sister. Well, at least I thought I didn't. But Cleo's been saying, 'Save me, Bertie' over and over, and she knows who I really am because she calls me 'Chef'—"

"Cleo can talk?" my mother interrupted.

"She *can't* talk, she's a flour sack! But I've got to save her, at least until I can bring her to class, then afterward I think we should all go see Dr. Zimmerman together and maybe find out if there's some special therapy group for people like us, you know, for flour sacks who pretend to be kids and the families who believe them, but until then, all I really need is to get Cleo to class to be graded." I gasped for breath.

"Mrs. Menendez is going to grade Cleo?" my mother asked. "Isn't that, well, severe? After all, you're an eighth grader and Cleo's a . . . a . . . "

"A flour sack!" I roared. I ran my fingers through my hair. I was never going to be able to explain this right. I tried another tactic. "Mom, Dad. Listen carefully. Nicholas Dekker kidnapped Cleo. Can you help me save her?"

"Kidnapped?!" they both shrieked again.

They jumped out of bed.

"Quick, Bert, get dressed while I call the police!" My father punched 911 into his cell phone.

"No police!" I snatched the phone and cancelled the call. "The . . . the kidnapper's note said to come alone . . . or else."

At those ominous words, my parents looked at each other. My mother's eyes started to fill up. Then she shook her head a little, frowned, and massaged her temples.

"But wait a minute," she began. "I mean, Cleo isn't—"

"Mom," I pleaded. "*Who*ever she is, *what*ever she is, however she got here, Cleo needs us, all of us, right now. Please?"

"You're right," my father said solemnly. "We've got to do it for Cleo."

"For Cleo," I agreed. We both looked at my mother. There was a very long pause.

Finally she smiled a bit, then nodded half a bit. "For Cleo."

Fifteen minutes later, with just a hint of dawn in the sky, we were ringing Dekker's doorbell.

Suddenly I wondered, What were we going to say?

Mrs. Dekker answered. She was no longer the dynamo who only yesterday transformed our class into a court-room. Now she had half-closed eyes and a bad case of bed head, and on her feet were pink bunny slippers.

"Wha—?" she asked. "Who has the nerve to ring my bell before my first cup of coffee?" She squinted at me. "Oh, the flour-sack boy," she murmured, closing her eyes again.

"So *you're* in on it, too," my mother said.

"In on what?"

From the door came the smell of Mocha Java coffee mingled with the scent of something cooking.

"Where is she?" I demanded.

"Who?"

"Cleo!" answered my father.

"Who's Cleo?" asked Mrs. Dekker.

Embarrassment, heavy as a blanket, seemed to drop on us from the sky. My parents shuffled their feet. What bad timing for a reality check!

"She's my flour sack," I explained. "My special project,

my key to high school." Nothing seemed to penetrate her fog. "She's my baby!" I blurted out. "Cleo's my baby and I've got to save her!"

"From what?"

"Your son. He kidnapped her yesterday while you and I were in the office saying nice things to each other. Maybe you *are* in on it."

One eye peeked open. "Nicky did what?"

"What are you cooking?" Maybe I could get her to slip and confess.

"I'm brewing coffee. Coffee. I need my coffee," she mumbled.

"What else?"

"I don't need anything else, just my coffee."

"No, what else are you cooking?"

"Huh? Oh, waffles." The one eye closed. "To go with my coffee."

"Waffles?" My mother's lower lip started to tremble.

"Frozen or homemade?" I asked.

"Young man," Mrs. Dekker said, trying to open both eyes at once. "What possible business do you have with my waffles?"

"They might be my sister."

"What?"

"Frozen or homemade?" My mother elbowed past me and grabbed the collar of Mrs. Dekker's bathrobe. "Frozen or homemade?!"

"Frozen! Now *shoo*!" Mrs. Dekker stepped from the door to wave us away. "All I want is a cup of coffee or two, maybe three, not twenty questions. And you people–" She turned her scrunched-up face toward my mother's voice. "What sort of parent comes along on a prank like this?"

"What sort of parent?" I repeated. I felt the heat rise up my neck and make my brain simmer. "Nobody calls my parents 'what sort of parent.' Besides, what sort of parent condones torture, kidnap, the destruction of the sacred family unit?"

"Who's been kidnapped?" Mrs. Dekker asked.

The solution I'd been looking for was finally obvious.

"You!" I shouted.

At last, both sleepy eyes popped open at once. "Me?" She took a step backward.

I grabbed her hand. "No, not really, don't go–just listen to me. *Your* son took *my* flour sack. I can't graduate without it."

"Nicky? My little Nicky?"

"Your little Nicky–" Is a future #1 on the FBI's Most Wanted List, I wanted to say. But I had to be diplomatic. "He . . . he has issues."

"Issues?" Her eyes bulged and her cheeks turned pale.

"Yes, issues. He needs help fast, *I* need help fast, and you're the only one who can help us both."

I tugged on her hand gently.

"I know a place where we can talk about Nicky, and

where there's lots and lots and *lots* of coffee," I said. "I promise you the biggest cup they have."

She glanced back at her house.

"Mocha Java," I said softly. "French Roast. Espresso shots. Doubles."

She nodded once, sharply. "Okay, let's talk."

She took the lead down the walk to our car.

"Bert!" cried my dad, hurrying to catch up. "Where on earth are you going?"

"To arrange an exchange of hostages."

DAY TEN—CONTINUED

After circling the Dunkin' Donuts three times to make sure there were no cops taking their break, my father pulled into the drive-thru and put in an order. Takeout in hand, we parked at the rear of the lot. I switched seats with my mother, going from the back with Mrs. Dekker to the front with my father. Then I made my call on the car phone and hit the speaker button. When a sleepy-voiced Dekker answered on the fifth ring, we could all hear him.

"Whosit?" he muttered.

"Notice anyone missing?" I asked.

"Wha—? Bertha, is that you? What's that?" he asked, suddenly awake. The phone clattered to the floor, and he was gone. In the background, I heard the shrill blast of a smoke detector.

Burnt waffles, I thought with satisfaction.

After a few minutes, the alarm stopped. As soon as

I heard him pick up the receiver, I demanded, "Where's Cleo?"

"She's gone, you pathetic loser! She was gonna be my breakfast. Now she's toast, thanks to you."

"Ha! Your mother already told us those waffles were frozen. Try again."

"My mother? What about my mother?"

"We've got her."

"I don't believe you."

"Then where is she?"

"She must have left for work already." His voice was sullen. "I don't know and I don't care."

"Mmmmm!" Mrs. Dekker squealed. A big sip of Colombian roast prevented her from voicing her anger. *"Mmmmmmm!"*

Mrs. Dekker's garbled voice gave me an idea.

"That's your mother through the gag," I said. "I want my flour sack, Nicky-poo."

"Don't call me that!"

"What, Nicky-poo? Shorty? Small fry? Your mother's been kidnapped and you're worrying about nicknames?"

"Go ahead, keep her."

At that, Mrs. Dekker swallowed wrong and began to choke. My mother, sitting next to her, thumped loudly on her back while the poor woman coughed.

"Do you hear that?" I asked. "Things could get very ugly here."

"What are you doing to her?"

"You don't want to know," I said menacingly. "Listen, you've got Cleo, I've got your mother. From here on in, it's simple."

"Oh yeah? Maybe your little baby's not waffles. But how do you know she's not bread, huh? A nice big loaf just waiting to be sliced!"

My mother gasped. Mrs. Dekker made comforting shushing noises.

"Cleo's safe," I said. And she was. Somehow I just knew it. "But if I don't get her back, if I fail eighth grade, or if anything happens to her, I swear I'll—"

"What? You'll bake a cake? I'll tell you right now, my mother's favorite is double chocolate."

Angrily, Mrs. Dekker made a grab for the phone. She moved so fast, coffee sloshed out of the cup, turning her pink bunny slippers brown.

"Ooohhhhh!" she wailed.

"All right, all right!" Dekker said. "I'll do it! Just leave my mother alone!"

"Twenty minutes," I told him. "The Market Street bridge."

"No, eight-fifteen at . . . at Overlook Park."

"Twenty minutes," I insisted.

"I can't, that's too early."

I had a sudden flash of clarity, the kind I wished would come during a math test but never did.

I knew where Cleo was.

"Eight o'clock," I said. "The schoolyard. Right outside the eighth-grade class."

There was a very long silence.

"Okay." He hung up the phone.

I looked at my waiting parents.

"Cleo's still in school," I said. "She's been there all along."

"So she was never really kidnapped?" asked my mother.

"Not kidnapped, *hidden*." I guess Dekker and I had been mortal enemies so long I was beginning to think like him. "If he really got rid of Cleo," I explained, "I could blame him and there would be a chance I might be believed. Then he would get in trouble. But if I blamed him and Cleo later turned up, it would look like I had lost her. Then I would be irresponsible because I had lost my baby, a liar for trying to hide it, and a creep for blaming it on him. I would fail for sure, and Dekker would get away with the whole thing."

Fully awake at last, Mrs. Dekker shook her head.

"I never would have thought my dear sweet little Nicky could be so mean," she said sadly. "How can I help? What do we do now?"

I looked at the empty donut bag as my father guiltily licked his fingers. "There's just enough time for another drive-thru order," I said. "Then we go back to the house so I can get ready for school."

The last bell had rung, and the stragglers were inside. I stood alone in the schoolyard, my knapsack in hand. Sunlight slanted in my eyes, but instead of being blinded, I saw everything more sharply: the crisscross of the chain-link fencing, the white cement between every brick, the pockmarked grains of blacktop beneath my feet. A snapped branch hushed the birds to silence. My hands twitched. I was Luke Skywalker facing Darth Vader.

I stood outside my class, while Mrs. Dekker waited with my parents, hidden in the bushes at the side of the schoolyard. Because of the glaring reflection, I couldn't really see into the room; then a face appeared at the glass, and a second, and a third, and through the open windows, I heard whispers. For the briefest instant, I thought I saw Indra. The image vanished like a ghost.

About halfway down the school, one of the doors opened and Dekker appeared, backpack slung over his shoulder. He began to walk toward me. I wanted to rush up and punch him in the face. I could do it, too, I thought; I had discovered that this week. But that wasn't *my* way. Besides, how could I make rose garnishes out of tomato skins if I had a broken hand?

Behind me, I heard another door open, close, then open again. Though I didn't turn to check, I bet Indra had taken one look out the window, then come out to help. And I bet Mrs. M. had followed.

Everyone in my life was here, I realized, everyone who meant anything to me, good or bad.

"Where's my mother?" Dekker asked, throwing his knapsack down.

"Where's Cleo?" I countered, throwing down mine.

He unzipped his backpack, took out a flour sack, and held it up. It was Cleo–lolling tongue, crossed eyes, Band-Aid on her forehead. Pulling the bag close, Dekker worked his finger under the bottom flap and threatened to spill Cleo's innards all over the yard.

Hands trembling, I unzipped my pack, unzipped the inner pocket, and took out my chef's hat. I fluffed up the toque and, like a king crowning himself, carefully pulled it onto my head. It was a perfect fit. If I went down today, I'd go down cooking.

Dekker was startled into speech.

"What is *that*?"

"What do you think, you idiot? It's a chef's hat. It's called a toque."

"It makes you look like the Pillsbury Dough Boy, Bertha."

"I *am* the Pillsbury Dough Boy!" My cheeks flamed. I shouted the words anyway, shouted loudly enough for everyone to hear. "I'm a *chef! A cook! A baker!* You'd better give me that flour sack right now, Dekker. She belongs in the hands of a trained professional."

"First, Dough Boy, where's my mother?"

My eyes almost flickered toward the bushes. Clearly

visible lined up beneath the greenery were a pair of black wingtips, a pair of white sneakers, and a pair of bunny slippers, mottled pink and brown. I had been afraid that the bunny slippers would dash out any second, but they hadn't. And now I knew why they hadn't moved.

Mrs. Dekker *wanted* to be ransomed.

"Maybe I'll keep your mother," I told Dekker. "She was pretty cool yesterday in class."

He started to rip open the bottom flap. A trickle of white dusted the ground. I kept talking.

"It doesn't matter anymore what you do," I said. It was true. Mrs. M. could see he had taken Cleo, so I should get those three extra points and pass. And I had declared I was a chef. What was left? I seemed to hear a faint whisper: *Just me.*

"You can't keep my mother!" Dekker said.

"Why not?"

"You just can't!" He looked exasperated. "Besides, what would you *do* with her?"

I shrugged. "I don't know. It wouldn't be so bad, having two moms. You know, double a good thing. Why do *you* want her back?"

"She's my mother! And I–"

"You what?"

"I . . . I . . ." He turned red. No words came out.

I couldn't believe it. Could Nick Dekker have a weakness after all, one more vulnerable than being called

"Shorty"? Could it truly be his mother? Did he deep down–better make that deep, *deep* down–feel something for her besides the embarrassment he had shown so far? Or did he want her back just because it was practical? A bully like him could use a good lawyer in the family.

"Yes?" I prompted.

He still couldn't get beyond "I . . . I . . . "

"You what, Nicky?" Indra asked from behind me.

"I guess I . . ." His voice dropped lower. "I . . . "

Mrs. Dekker couldn't wait a second longer. A stammer and a blush were enough for her.

"You love me!" she declared, and burst out of the bushes.

A dozen girly voices sighed, "Awwwww," from the classroom windows.

I grabbed Mrs. Dekker by the wrist and dragged her back. She had to wait till I made the exchange. Slowly we walked toward Dekker, closer and closer, step by step, inch by inch. Everything was going as planned, until Mrs. Dekker broke free and leapt toward her son.

When his mother launched herself, Dekker stumbled back. His hand shot up and he let go of Cleo. Up, up, up she flew! I dived to catch her, getting only too good a look at her bottom, the flap turned the wrong way–out and now ripped fully open.

In my Jedi-knight clarity, I saw everything in slow motion as Cleo finally fell to earth, just inches from my outstretched fingers. *Oof!* She landed as gracefully as a flour sack can land under such undignified circumstances. The impact made the loose flour that had already spilled out puff up into a cloud that spread over everything. Was it magic, the wind, or just a drop in blood sugar that made the whole hot June world suddenly seem sprinkled with snow?

A second later, Mrs. Dekker was hugging her son. And Dekker, black hair now powdered, was actually hugging her back.

"That was *sooo* nice what you did for Nicky's mom," Indra said from behind me. I turned. Indra's hair, too, was shot through with white. She leaned over and gave me a quick kiss. From the windows came another chorus of "Awwwwww."

"It was nothing," I said, trying not to faint. "I mean, the poor lady needs some help; she's got Nick Dekker for a kid."

"And I've got you."

There they were, my mother and my father, all rumpled from crawling through the bushes. Bits of twigs and leaves stuck to their clothes.

"Young man," my mother said. There was something weird in her voice. It took a minute, then I knew what it was: Her voice was stern and all, all *momlike*. I had heard voices just like it on TV, but never in person.

"Bertie, you're grounded."

"Grounded?" It was a word from a foreign-language

dictionary, maybe trans-meso-Siberian or something, certainly nothing *I* had ever heard before. What terrible ideas had Mrs. Dekker been feeding my mother while they were in the bushes? "What do you mean I'm grounded?"

She gave an exaggerated sigh; obviously my being grounded was the clearest fact in the whole world.

"Bertie, kidnapping is a federal offense."

"It wasn't really kidnapping," I sputtered. "It was really just . . . just luring away with coffee."

"But her son truly believed that—"

"You can't ground me!" I yelled. "Summer's coming!"

The idea of my mother disciplining me was dizzying. I was bending over to put my head between my knees and breathe deep, when I felt a firm tap on my shoulder. I straightened up. It was Mrs. Menendez with her grade book. Flour dusted her navy-suited shoulders.

She held out one hand.

I gently picked up Cleo, held the flap closed, and handed her over.

Mrs. M. looked at Cleo this way and that way, top to bottom, side to side. She nodded once, returned her, and opened the grade book. With a frown, she blew a puff of white from its pages, then made a mark in the book.

"You passed."

Indra and I both jumped into the air and whooped.

"Now, tell me, Mr. Hooks," Mrs. M. said. "Have you learned a lesson from this?"

My answer was immediate: "That parents, and maybe even all adults, are generally clueless when it comes to kids?"

"No," Mrs. M. said sharply. "Try again."

"That, um . . . " I tried to think fast and talk slowly. "That kids shouldn't be . . . embarrassed by their parents, um, because *everyone's* parents are embarrassing?"

"No!"

What did she want from me? I saw Nicky at the end of the schoolyard and remembered how this whole thing had started.

"That kids are always the creepiest to other kids?"

"No, Mr. Hooks! I'm talking about discovering that even *you* are capable of responsibility and can succeed."

"Oh. Well, if success means being able to inspire the first Nobel Prize in Cooking, then, yes, I'll succeed." I grinned. I had actually said that out loud.

"Don't worry, Mrs. Menendez," said my father. "We're seeing a therapist. In fact, the three of us have an appointment this evening."

"The three of us?" I asked. "Mom, me . . . and Cleo?"

My mother and father exchanged a worried look. Then my mother said very gently, "Dr. Zimmerman asked to see all three of us, remember? But, of course, you can bring Cleo, too, if you want." She tousled my hair, then turned to Mrs. Menendez and said, "Thank you so much for everything. See you Tuesday?"

"Yes, I'll be there."

I was puzzled. "Be where?"

"The past-life regression class we both attend," Mrs. M. said.

"Past . . . life . . . regression?" That explained why my mother had remembered her that day on Church Street. "You, too, Mrs. M.?" I asked. The last little bit of the sane world turned upside down as I imagined possible past lives for her.

I was still hyperventilating when my mother said, "Bertie, after the doctor tonight, I thought, maybe, um, you might, um, show me how to cook."

"You, cook?" I could already see the results: food poisoning or starvation.

"I think I'd like to try, if you'll teach me," she said. "I've noticed you seem to have a little knack for it."

"A little knack? Most people won't be eating crème brûlée at home tonight. I'm a really, really good cook, Mom. I'm going to be a chef."

"I guess it's better than a spy."

"Which reminds me," my father said. "Crème brûlée is my boss's favorite. Would you mind if I brought him home sometime?"

"Home?"

"For you to cook for him."

Me cook for Dad's boss? What was the probability of that?

"Sure. Did you want me to help you land a big promotion?"

My father frowned. "No, but he's very friendly with the people at Wharton. I figure, he has four years to convince them to add cooking to the college courses. Like your mother said, you do seem to have a little knack for it. You could major in actuarial science and minor in cooking."

Minor in cooking. It was progress.

"Or we can get takeout," my father added. "Either or."

I guess being weird is an inescapable part of my family. That was okay with me. Just the sight of my parents, as they walked away, picking the twigs off each other's clothes, made something inside me squeeze tight, and I knew, if it came to it, that I would pay any ransom for them any day.

"Bertie," Indra asked. "Can you cook Indian food, like curries?"

"Curries and biryanis and vindaloo, but I don't have a clay oven for tandoori," I said.

"We do. Come over this weekend." She grinned. "My grandmother would love to meet you. All *I* ever do is boil and burn."

Then Mrs. M. sent Indra back to class, and it was just the two of us.

"So, Mr. Hooks, it's been quite a week, hasn't it?"

I nodded, dazed.

"What you said about children being nasty to their

peers," she continued, "there's usually a reason for it. Mr. Dekker, for example. He's moving next week."

That got my attention. "What?"

"I said he's moving—to Oshkosh. His mother has accepted a partnership with a new law firm, and his father will be commuting back and forth every weekend, at least till he gets a job there, too. Young Mr. Dekker is not very happy with his parents' decision."

But I was. I had wanted him kidnapped by aliens. I guess moving to Oshkosh was a close second.

"So many changes," Mrs. M. murmured. "Even for me."

"What do you mean?"

"My transfer came through this morning."

And then Mrs. Menendez smiled her very special I'm-so-pleased-with-myself smile, the one that usually meant I was in big trouble.

"I'll be teaching at the high school next year, Mr. Hooks. Do keep up with math over the summer. I expect we'll meet again."

Following Mrs. M. inside, Cleo in the crook of my arm, I realized that I had gotten everything I had asked for in Dr. Zimmerman's office. Indra had kissed me, my mom had acted like a mom, my dad had accepted me for who I was for at least a few minutes, I had passed eighth grade, and Nick Dekker was about to disappear. I had also announced to the world that I was a chef. All that other stuff—being star of a prime-time cooking show, owner of a four-star restaurant, author of a best-selling cookbook, and proprietor of a bed-and-breakfast—maybe I wouldn't, *couldn't,* do all those things. But whatever I did, I knew I was going to have a whisk in my hand.

I looked down at Cleo, cradled in my arms. She was smeared with dirt, and her bag was slack, only half full. But she was still my responsibility, still my little flour-sack baby. A bit of extra flour from the non-talking bag at home, some tape, and she would be okay. I knew the perfect corner in my room, where she would have a good view and not feel left out, on a small, soft pillow so she would be comfy. Maybe even with time, her eyes would uncross.

After all, in a way I owed her everything.

This sounds something like, "Just do it," but it isn't. Writing is never easy, but if you don't actually sit down, and actually try, and actually squeeze out even just a word or two, nothing at all gets written. A sentence a day eventually adds up to something, but nothing a day adds up to nothing each and every time. Also, more best advice is that every first draft stinks. That doesn't mean you're bad, only that the piece needs to be rewritten—like every other piece in the world by every other writer in the world.

What do you wish you could do better?
Everything, including write.

When you finish a book, who reads it first?
My critique group. My family never reads my work—at all—whether in manuscript form or published. It would be very awkward if they didn't like something or if I thought they were totally crazy in their comments.

Are you a morning person or a night owl?
I used to be a night owl, then somewhere along the way I became a morning person, and somewhere further along the way, I've become a 10:00 A.M. to 10:15 A.M. person.

What makes you laugh out loud?
No so much a what but a who. My husband is very funny and makes me laugh out loud, which is one of the reasons I married him.

Which do you like better: cats or dogs?
Neither. I'm a bird person through and through. I have two parrots, an African Jardine and an African Grey. They're called, respectively, Wallace and Gromit, after the British claymation characters. I didn't name them myself and would have picked something else, especially in retrospect. "Gromit" is not a real name for a real person.

How did you celebrate publishing your first book?
I actually don't remember. But that's nothing new. I have a terrible memory. For example, and I am not making this up, I don't remember being proposed to. My husband says it was very romantic. He proposed to me in a holly tree forest in one of the state parks. I have absolutely no memory of that at all. But I guess he did, because suddenly we were planning our wedding.

What do you value most in your friends?
Honesty, a sense of humor, and undying admiration of my brilliance.

What time of year do you like best?
Winter, as long as it doesn't snow too much. A cold dry winter is best.

What's your favorite TV show?
House, or as my son calls it, Dr. Dreamy McDreamy.

What's the best advice you have ever received about writing?
That writers write. They don't just think about writing.

GOFISH

SUSAN HEYBOER O'KEEFE

When did you realize you wanted to be a writer?
I "was" a writer as soon as I could literally write, which was about age five, and so never thought about it. I already just "was." For me, writing has always been as natural—and as absolutely necessary—as breathing. As far as the business of trying to get published, I started submitting and collecting rejection slips when I was thirteen and got my first acceptance when I was nineteen.

What's your first childhood memory?
Standing on a chair at the stove, stirring tapioca.

What was your worst subject in school?
Penmanship and geography in a dead heat.

What was your first job?
When I was about ten, a friend and I wrote and published a local newspaper and sold it by subscription to the neighbors.